7/24/2014

To ~~Margaret~~ Martha Chase and her husband with my best personal regards. It has been a

# Their Unbridled Rivalry

pleasure meeting both of you. I hope you enjoy reading

by

my novel and watching The

### Walter Jensen, MD

movie when it is produced.

*Walter Jensen, MD*

D1728274

TELEMACHUS PRESS

This book is a work of fiction. Names, characters, places and incidents are either the product of the author's imagination or are used fictitiously. Any resemblance to actual persons, living or dead, or to actual events or locales is entirely coincidental.

**THEIR UNBRIDLED RIVALRY**

The publisher does not have any control over and does not assume any responsibility for author or third-party websites or their content.

Cover designed by Telemachus Press, LLC

Cover art:
Copyright © iStock/000007738694/buzbuzzer
Copyright © iStock/000019878445/mphillips007
Copyright © iStock/000020817808/GlobalP
Copyright © iStock/000026097281/Yuri_Arcurs
Copyright © iStock/000027951634/CentralITAlliance

Published by Telemachus Press, LLC
http://www.telemachuspress.com

Visit the author website:
http://www.walterjensenmd.com

ISBN: 978-1-940745-21-3 (eBook)
ISBN: 978-1-940745-22-0 (Paperback)

Version 2013.12.27

Printed in the United States of America

10  9  8  7  6  5  4  3  2  1

# Dedication

*To Carolyn, Jack, and James.*

# Acknowledgements

I am grateful for the excellent English professors at Williams College in Williamstown, Massachusetts who generously helped me in my quest to learn and to improve my writing skills. I was so fortunate to be awarded the generous seven-year Tyng scholarship from Williams College. It basically covered all my expenses at Williams and for my first three years at Stanford. I extend my deepest thanks to Williams College and the Tyng Foundation for that honor and for the opportunities the scholarship afforded me.

I would also like to acknowledge my Stanford School of Medicine professors who were brilliant and stimulating educators and researchers. It was a privilege to study under them. They brought out the very best in me and I am deeply indebted to them. They also encouraged me to continue on a path of lifelong learning and to sustain an unquenchable curiosity. Stressing the importance of high ethical standards, compassion, responsibility and empathy, they were highly influential in the way I approached caring for patients.

My professors during my residency and fellowship training programs were also exceptional and they encouraged excellence in research and patient care.

I am grateful for the help of Steve Jackson, Stephanie Kunz and the cover artist, Johnny Breeze, all hailing from Telemachus Press for moving "Their Unbridled Rivalry" through to publication.

I want to extend my heartfelt thanks to Greg Berg for constructing such an excellent website for me.

Special thanks go out to Bart DiLiddo, PhD and Linda Royer at VectorVest. They were kind enough to let me highlight their stock analysis and portfolio management system in my novel.

I want to acknowledge all of the resorts, wineries, restaurants, and specialty services in Napa Valley who extended me the privilege of including them in "Their Unbridled Rivalry."

I'm grateful for all the support I received from the physicians, nurses, executives, and staff of the Scripps Clinic and Green Hospital in La Jolla, California. We shared a camaraderie and culture unique to a large multi-specialty group. Finally I want to thank my colleagues in the Chest and Critical Care division especially Robert Sarnoff, Arthur Dawson, Larry Kline and Rick Timms. I appreciated their leadership, intellectual stimulation, outstanding patient care and friendship. It was a privilege to be associated with them.

# Their Unbridled Rivalry

# Chapter 1

THE LOUDSPEAKER IN the hospital barked. "Dr. Russell rush immediately to room 417 west." Running up the stairs he burst into the hospital room to find an attractive middle aged woman clutching her chest. "Mrs. Valerie Goldin had a right total knee replacement by Dr. Creighton yesterday and just started to complain of severe chest pain a few moments ago," the nurse said. "Get an electrocardiogram while I talk to her. Where is the pain Mrs. Goldin?" "It's just to the left of my mid chest," she said. "Does it hurt to take a deep breath?" he asked. "No, it's just a steady pain and it's getting worse," she said clutching her chest. The EKG tech rushed into the room and quickly hooked her up to the electrocardiogram machine. Dr. Russell took a careful look at the heart tracing and said. "It's a problem with your heart Mrs. Goldin." He turned to the nurse and said. "Place her on 6 Liters of nasal oxygen and give her 4 milligrams of intramuscular morphine. Prepare to transfer her to the cardiac catheterization lab. Mrs. Goldin you are having an acute heart attack and we must try to open the coronary artery that is blocked as soon as possible." Valerie was terrified. "A heart attack!" she exclaimed. "I'm too young to have a heart attack." She had never before faced the possibility of death and experienced a moment of panic. Grasping her husband's arm, she asked with concern in her voice. "What can be done?" "I will ask our best interventional cardiologist, Dr. Daniel Friedman to perform an emergency coronary angiogram on you. He is one of the best in the country and is fortunately here in the hospital," he said. Leaving the room Dr. Russell had Dr. Friedman paged stat. Dr.

Friedman answered immediately. "Dan we have a Mrs. Valerie Goldin in need of an emergency coronary angiogram. She's having a major myocardial infarction. Yesterday she had a right total knee replacement by Dr. Creighton. I thought we would be dealing with an acute blood clot to her lungs, but that's not the case. Can I meet you in the cath room in five minutes?" he asked. "Absolutely, Bill. Are her relatives here?" he asked. "Yes her husband and parents are here."

Charles, Valerie's husband was visibly shaken. Fear registered on his face. His hands were shaking. He felt helpless. "You're going to make it Valerie," he said, but he was frightened. Dr. Russell reappeared and with the help two nurses Valerie was transferred to a gurney for transportation to the cath lab. "Will she make it Dr. Russell?" he asked. "If Dr. Friedman can unblock the coronary artery quickly, she should do very well," he replied. "And if he can't what will happen?" Charles asked. "Let's first see what he can accomplish," he said. Valerie realized that every minute made a difference. She was struggling with her emotions as she was being wheeled down to the cath lab. She was anxious to get going.

Her parents had flown down to San Diego from northern California to lend support to Valerie during her right total knee replacement. They were overwhelmed by this turn of events, but her father tried to reassure her as they moved toward the cath lab. "Valerie one of my best friends had a heart attack two months ago. The 911 team rushed him to the Stanford University Medical Center where he had the blocked coronary artery opened up and a stent placed. He suffered no heart damage and resumed playing tennis at age 76 two weeks ago. So hang in there," he said. "The modern day cardiologists can perform miracles." Valerie hoped for a miracle. She wanted to play tennis again. Right now she would be happy just to survive. "Thanks for telling me that story. At least I have a head start on your friend. My heart attack is occurring while I'm in the hospital. That should make my chances for survival better, shouldn't it, Dr. Russell?" she asked. "Yes it does. You have at least a thirty minute advantage and that can make all the difference in the world," he said trying to reassure her. The morphine was easing her chest pain and she experienced hope. She would soon be in the capable hands of Dr. Friedman.

Arriving in the cardiac cath lab Dr. Friedman introduced himself to Valerie and her relatives. Glancing at the EKG, he explained the procedure to them. "I'll thread a catheter up through a large artery in your groin and inject dye into the coronary arteries that supply your heart with blood. When I identify the blockage I'll place the catheter through the obstruction and inflate a tiny balloon to open it up. Then I'll place a small stent into the opened coronary artery to act as a scaffold to maintain the opening. Do you have any questions?" he asked. "How many of these procedures have you performed doctor?" Valerie asked. "Over 1000 and the vast majority of them have been extremely successful," he replied. "Complications can occur, but they're rare and I can deal with them should they arise."

Within an hour the coronary angiogram had been completed. It demonstrated a blockage of the left anterior descending coronary artery which supplied blood to a major portion of her heart. The balloon angioplasty and stent placement had been successfully performed. The electrocardiogram had returned toward normal. She was transferred to a coronary care room in the Intensive Care Unit. Shortly thereafter Dr. Friedman arrived. "I have very good news for you Mrs. Goldin," he said. "The operation was completely successful. You should do very well." She looked up at him with tears in her eyes and said. "Thank you doctor. I was so fortunate to have you here in the hospital when this happened wasn't I?" she said. "Yes you were," he said. "The blockage was in the main left coronary artery that leads to the left side of your heart. That blockage is called a widow maker or in your case a widower maker. I had to unblock it rapidly or a major part of your heart would have died. I think I accomplished that and you should do very well."

Charles and her parents celebrated. "I was so worried Valerie," Charles said. "But you've made it." Her parents were also visibly relieved. "Isn't it incredible what modern technology and well trained doctors can accomplish," her father said. He was so thankful. "I had such a foreboding feeling before the operation took place," Valerie said. "Visions of my life flashed in front me. I suddenly realized what meant the most to me. It was the special people in my life. I also realized what a terrible relationship I'm having with Jason Gianelli, my rival in the office. The stress involved in dealing with him is eating away at my life. At least I am alive to defend my clients from his greedy grasp." Her parents were shocked. They had no idea that Valerie was in some kind of toxic relationship with one of her co-workers at the Robert Kaplan investment Services firm in La Jolla California where she worked as an investment advisor. "Is he really that bad?" her mother asked. "He's despicable mother," Valerie replied. "He tries to steal my clients on a regular basis and criticizes my investment strategies. He's always touting his superior investment returns through his option seminars. At first I was just annoyed, but now he's making me angry." Charles was alarmed. "Please, Valerie, try to relax and forget about Jason. Don't get worked up over him." he said. "I'm going to arrange a victory party for you, your parents and your friends. After this frightening experience, we have reason to celebrate." Valerie smiled. "Yes we do. I'll look forward to a party." It had been a harrowing day, but it was having a beautiful ending.

"It's time that I leave the hospital and go home," Charles said. "Is there anything I can do for you, Valerie before I leave?" "Yes, when you get home please give Sasha a big hug for me. Then tomorrow sneak her into my hospital room" she replied. "I'm sure she misses me." Sasha was their prized Yorkshire terrier. They had adopted her six years earlier. She was a bundle of energy and enlivened the Goldin's lives on a daily basis. Before she became crippled by her right knee injury Valerie had exercised Sasha every morning and evening. She had also established herself as Sasha's pack leader by not letting Sasha run in front of her. Obedience and discipline were key ingredients in training a dog and Sasha had been trained well by Valerie. Over the years Valerie and Sasha had bonded and they clearly loved each other. Some people doubt that dogs can experience love, but Valerie thought they were wrong. Perhaps affection described their relationship better than love. Whatever it was they had formed a powerful attachment.

Charles wondered just how much Sasha missed Valerie. Valerie had only been gone for two days. "Sasha is moping around the house, Valerie. She gives me a quizzical look when I returned home without you. Maybe I'm only imagining it. Do dogs really miss their owner after only two days of absence?" "Of course they do," Valerie said. In fact Valerie believed that the speed with which Sasha wagged her tail was a direct measurement of how much she cared. Whenever Sasha came in contact with Valerie her tail would start to wag like a revved up car windshield wiper.

Dr. Friedman returned to inquire into Valerie's medical history. "I wonder why you had a premature heart attack Mrs. Goldin. I see from your birthday that you just turned 50 on June 1, 2010. That was only only 12 days ago. You seem to be in excellent health other than your bad knee. Is there a history of heart disease in your family?" he asked. "My paternal grandfather died of a heart attack at 65 and my maternal grandmother who also died of a heart attack at 67. They were both very heavy cigarette smokers. You met both of my parents. They are alive and well in their 70's. My older brother is 56 and has no known heart disease," she replied. "Do you have a history of high blood pressure, diabetes, smoking cigarettes or bad blood lipids like a high cholesterol?" he asked. "No, not to my knowledge. I've never smoked and don't take any medications other than acetaminophen and ibuprofen for pain in my right knee. Before the knee surgery I was carefully evaluated by my internist, Dr. Rebecca Wright, and she said that everything was fine except for an elevated LDL cholesterol of 135. I have been an athlete all my life and played competitive tennis at Stanford on the women's tennis team. Until the knee stopped me, I was working out of the gym three times a week and I've always been careful to avoid fatty foods." "Well I am surprised that you had a heart attack. What is your occupation?" he asked. "I'm a financial advisor with the Kaplan Investment Services here in La Jolla," she replied. "Is the job stressful?" Dr. Friedman asked. She cringed at the question. "Yes, I suppose it is. It's a very competitive business and I'm paid a commission based on the size of my client accounts. Trying to grow those accounts only comes when you provide your clients with acceptable financial returns," she said. Her husband intervened and beaming said. "Valerie is the second highest account holder in the firm. Her average return over the past 24 years with the company has been 12 percent per year. That's a record that's hard to beat!" Dr. Friedman whistled and said. "That's for sure. I think I'll turn my account over to you. Would you accept me as a client?" he asked. "It would be a privilege to manage your investments," she said. "If it takes a heart attack to gain you as a client, I guess this was my lucky day."

After he left, Valerie ruminated to herself. What I failed to tell him was that my competing partner, Jason Gianelli was my source of stress. Jason was the one with a 16.6 percent annualized return over the past 24 years.

They had both joined the firm in the same year, 1986. He was the options whiz kid from the Chicago option pits who had left the cold winter months of Chicago to bathe in the sunshine of San Diego. He possessed a gigantic ego and constantly reminded Valerie of her inadequate investment returns in comparison to his. He would take delight when a client of hers defected to him in search of better returns. In fact he actually tried to "steal" clients from her. By giving regular seminar talks extolling the virtues of options and shorting techniques he had managed to lure several of her best clients over to his side. To say she despised him would be mild she thought. Perhaps she even hated him and his arrogance. The inward seething she experienced almost every day most likely contributed to her heart attack. She knew she needed help in order to control her anger. She had been trying for years to do that on her own without success. Maybe she needed a psychiatrist to help her. She was just too proud to admit she needed a shrink. It took her several hours to fall asleep. The image of Jason Gianelli smiling when he learned she had suffered a heart attack kept her awake. She knew he would potentially use it as an excuse to persuade more of her clients to vacate to his stable of assets.

# Chapter 2

AS VALERIE WAS recovering from her transient heart attack and knee surgery in the La Jolla Hospital, Jason Gianelli was conducting an option trading seminar at the Robert Kaplan Investment Services office. He appeared vibrant and enthusiastic as he circled around in front of his audience. He stood erect and tall at six foot two inches and he weighed a solid and muscular 220 pounds. At 50 he was ruggedly handsome. Most of all he was smart. His presence was indeed impressive. His only physical flaw was a slight limp, the result of a college football injury.

"There are spectacular opportunities to generate excellent financial returns trading options in the current stock market," he said. Of the ten clients in attendance three were former clients of Valerie Goldin. "You have certainly proven that to us over the past year Mr. Gianelli," one of them said. "Right now there are certain sectors that I find extremely appealing," Jason said. "Give us an example," a client requested. "Certain stocks within the technology sector are rising steadily and for valid reasons," Jason said. "There's one computer company I particularly like. I have already placed a great deal of your money into buying its call options over the past year. Their innovations have been incredible. Their sales have been exuberant over the years. Profit margins have been high and their earnings have been exceptional. In just the past year their shares have risen from approximately $138 per share on June 11, 2009 to $266 on June 26, 2010. I think their share price will continue to rise and I have continued to buy in

the money call options with expiration dates 3 to 4 months into the future."
"Won't there be pull backs?" a client asked. "Yes, but I think the overall
trend is still up at least for the next year and perhaps longer. You must trust
me to exit a bullish option call strategy when I think it's appropriate to do
so. I have the flexibility to short a stock and buy put options if a stock starts
to decline in price. Those of you who have invested with me before 2007
know how successful I was in employing that strategy in 2007 through
2008," he said. "Yes your returns were amazing. Some of my friends were
watching their portfolios get decimated while you were making us money,"
a client said. "Yes, a few of you were investing with Valerie Goldin during
those two years," he said. "Her investments did rather poorly and I had two
excellent up years."

A distinguished looking gentleman stood up and announced. "That's
when I switched from her to you, Mr. Gianelli and I'm glad I did. I've made
a lot more money investing with you." Jason smiled. He loved it when
someone switched their account from Valerie over to him. "Well I will
continue to surpass her returns. She is just too conservative and her options
trades lack imagination," he said. "Money flows where money grows. I enjoy competing with her."

"I still have some of my assets with Valerie Goldin looking for a
steady, conservative return," a matronly woman said. "She refers to you as
the options wizard. I think she's jealous over your success." "She just sells
covered calls and puts," Jason said. "Valerie's training has led to a more
conservative form of investing. It has produced decent but not great returns. My option trading has led to significantly higher returns. Valerie and I
both compete for investment clients." "Valerie became very upset when I
switched most of my assets to you," the same lady replied. "She knows my
investment returns exceed hers," Jason said. "She shouldn't be surprised
when she loses clients to me. But remember successful option trading is
based upon leverage, pricing and timing. If you don't get those elements
right, your entire investment can vanish."

Of course Jason didn't mention his disastrous losses from the option
trades he had made during the "flash crash" of early 2010. Sudden reversals
in pharmaceutical and insurance stock prices had resulted in those call options expiring worthless. He also misjudged his timing on several bank and

technology stocks. Again those call options expired worthless. He anguished over those setbacks and knew he had to do better in the second half of 2010 to beat out Valerie. Now he would have to scramble to make up for those losses. He knew the stock market could be volatile. Usually he played the volatility inherent to stock options favorably, but not in these instances. Had Valerie been caught in the earlier 2010 downturn? He wasn't sure. She used a system that was far more conservative than his, but that meant her returns were usually more consistent and positive. He realized that he probably had some catching up to do if he was going to outclass Valerie's returns in 2010.

"How did you become such a successful option trader Jason?" a client asked. "I was very fortunate. One of the founders of the Option Exchange in Chicago had been a star running back on the 1956 Notre Dame Football team. As a staunch Notre Dame football alumnus, he had followed my own football career at Notre Dame. When I graduated in 1982 he offered me a job. He along with many others on the option exchange mentored me in option trading. They were among the most knowledgeable and successful option traders in the world," he said.

"In 1985 an Institute for Options was founded to help educate investors around the world about options. I attended many of those initial option seminars. While Valerie was attending the Stanford School of Business, my education came from my mentors and from attending option seminars. Put options were introduced in 1977 as away to hedge risk in trading stocks. I grasped the concept and have used it very successfully over the ensuing years."

"I don't fully understand put options. Can you explain them to me?" a client asked.

"Most people don't understand puts and put option strategies very well," Jason said. "When I buy a put option it gives me the right to sell 100 shares of a stock at a certain price called the strike price before it expires sometime in the future on the expiration date. It's the opposite of a call option which would give me the right to buy the stock at the strike price before it expires. It's called a put because it gives me the right to put or sell the stock to someone else. I buy put options when I think the price of a stock is going to go down. As the stock falls in price, the put option increases in value. Usually I just sell the highly appreciated put options before they expire." "How did you use puts to make us money in 2007 and 2008?" another client asked.

Jason looked intently at the option seminar participants. "I'll give you an example," he said. "On October 9, 2007 the stock price for one of the large banks was $53 per share. I thought it was overvalued and the price would fall. I bought 50 November 2007 puts with a strike price of $53 for $2 or $200 per contract of 100 shares. Buying 50 contracts gave me control of 5000 shares for a total cost of 50 times $200 dollars or $10,000 dollars. On November 9, 2007 the share price had fallen to $44 dollars. I sold my put options which had soared in value to $6 per contract of 100 shares. Since I controlled 5000 shares, I made $6 times 5000 or $30,000. Yes, it cost me $10,000, but I made $20,000 in just over a month. It's the leverage that trading options gives you that make them so attractive. Each $10,000 investment in buying the puts made me $20,000. That's an 200% return in just over a month!" "What a spectacular return," a client exclaimed. Jason stood up to his full height. He rocked back and forth smiling. He was proud of his brilliant trade.

"You have to remain flexible to make money," he said. "When quantitative easing and falling interest rates occurred in 2009, I reversed my option strategy and started buying calls on stocks I thought would rally. In fact many stocks did rally and I sold my call options before their expiration dates. Those trades were also quite profitable In 2009 on client accounts I managed worth $500,000 I made over $100,000 dollars on technology call options alone." He didn't mention the $40,000 dollars he lost on housing call options that expired worthless. He was talented, but he was far from perfect.

Jason's reputation for generating superior investment returns was being circulated throughout the San Diego investment community. He was gaining more clients. Valerie was unfortunately losing clients to him. The fact that he gloated when one of her clients defected to him upset her. At times he even announced in one of his option seminars that another one of Valerie's clients had left her and transfered their assets to him to manage. She agonized each time that happened. Competing with him was frustrating and it was adversely affecting her heart.

# Chapter 3

JASON WAS SENDING monthly support checks to his mother. She desperately needed the money. His father, Gino Gianelli, had become an abusive drunk after he lost his job as a foreman in one of the Pittsburgh steel mills in the early 1970's. He would return home from the local Irish pub inebriated and surly. Jason had learned to avoid any encounter with him by retreating to his bedroom. There he would agonize over the cries of his mother being beaten by his father downstairs. Jason's father would belt whip young Jason over minor disagreements. It was no surprise that Jason grew up to hate his father. He longed for the day when he could seek revenge. He loved his mother who was kind and supportive. Jason wondered why she stayed married to him.

Jason increased his body building routine in high school. He grew to stand over six feet tall and he developed an impressive and powerful physique. As a star halfback on his high school football team, he was an acclaimed local hero. His father had attended only one of Jason's football games and it ended up in a disaster. Gino had arrived at he stadium drunk and belligerent. As he lurched toward his wife in order to find his seat, he crunched on a series of people's toes. "Watch where you're stepping," someone screamed. "Get your ugly feet out of my way," Gino replied.

When Jason made a spectacular 35 yard run, Gino stood up, stumbled and dumped half of his cup of beer on Leroy Johnson who was sitting in front of him. Leroy was the African American father of one of Jason's closest friends on the football team. Leroy was also a burly man who had been an outstanding football tackle in his prime. "Watch what you're do-ing," Leroy said as he turned and glared directly at Gino looking for an apology. With utter disdain Gino only sneered and threw the rest of his beer into Leroy's face. That action infuriated Leroy and a bloody brawl en-sued. They were both eventually escorted out of the stadium by the police. As they left the stadium, they continued to hurl obscenities at one another. It was a humiliating experience for Jason and his mother. It only served to intensify the hatred Jason felt toward his father.

Later that evening Jason returned home after a date to see his father slapping his mother around in the living room. He took three steps forward and delivered a jaw shattering blow to his father's face. His father slumped to the floor and Jason stood over him menacingly. "If I ever see you strike her again, I will beat you to a pulp," he said. "If you want someone to fight, attack me and not my mother. I hate you," he exclaimed.

He tenderly wiped the tears from his mother's eyes and soothed her face with a wash cloth filled with crushed ice. That night his urge to leave home and Pittsburgh grew even stronger. He vowed that after he left he would never return. His mother's meager income as a local librarian was their major source of income. Jason made a vow that someday he would become rich. Then he would be able to provide financial support for his mother. He didn't care what happened to his father. He was a drunk and Jason was ashamed of him.

Encouraged by his loving and supportive mother, Jason studied hard and ended up fifth in his graduating high school class of 412 students. As a student athlete, he was avidly recruited by colleges and universities. Finally he decided to attend the University of Notre Dame on an academic schol-arship. There he starred as a running back on the Fighting Irish football team. Unfortunately, he was sidelined by a knee injury late in the season of his senior year. It left him with a slight limp, but it was barely noticeable.

Jason became passionate in his zeal to excel both academically and athletically at Notre Dame. His record there was outstanding. It was no surprise that he later become a stellar option trader on the Chicago Board Option Exchange. His determination and fierce competitive spirit accom-panied him to the Robert Kaplan Investment Services firm in 1986. There he would do whatever was required to become the most successful investment advisor in the firm. The drive to excel had become his overriding passion. He would even be willing to employ devious tactics to gain preeminence and a high commission income. He would finally be able to generously support his mother. He yearned to return the love and care she had shown him growing up. He thought the best way he could do that was by providing her with money.

He was so excited to hear her voice when she called. "Thank you, son, for sending us money. We will finally be able to pay our overdue bills. It's been such a struggle." "I'm glad I'm able to help out, mom. Be sure to buy yourself some nice clothes and a new winter coat," he said. "Will you have enough money left over to do that?" "With your generous check we'll have more than enough." "Then splurge a little, mom. You've never been able to do that. There will be more money coming next month." He could tell by her voice she was thrilled. "Thank you Jason. I love you son." "I love you too mom." "Well, you take care of yourself," she said. "Come visit us when you can get away. Good-bye and thanks again."

Jason was overjoyed. That interchange with his mother strengthened his drive to generate additional commission income.

His drunken father died in 1990 from alcoholic liver cirrhosis. Jason celebrated the day he died. No longer would any of his money support his father's drinking habits. He knew that his mother had been giving Gino drinking money. He postulated that that may have actually been good. It had probably served to accelerate Gino's death from cirrhosis.

Jason's co-workers would never understand the intensity of his love for his mother nor the intense hatred he felt toward his father. They would only observe his obsession to make money and lots of it.

# Chapter 4

VALERIE WAS TRANSFERRED to room 315 west in the La Jolla Hospital the following morning after her coronary stent placement. By the time the afternoon visiting hours ended her room was filled with flowers from grateful clients, co-workers and close friends. She was overwhelmed by the show of love and support. Tears filled her eyes as she read the wonderful get well cards. She beamed as her fellow investment advisors streamed into her room wishing her well. The one missing face was that of Jason Gianelli and she was glad. Robert Kaplan, the president of the Robert Kaplan Investment Services firm which employed her, entered her room smiling. "I'm so glad to see you recovering Valerie," he said. "I don't want to lose one of my star investment advisors." "Thanks for coming to see me Robert," Valerie replied. "It's only a temporary setback. I should be back at my office desk shortly." "Well, take your time," he said. "I want you to be fully recovered before you return to the office."

Valerie certainly had no intention of retiring during her prime earning years. Her client accounts had surpassed $15 million dollars last month. Earning a 0.015 commission on her total account base gave her a $225,000 per year income. She intended to make that grow. Investment advisors competed for clients and she enjoyed the process.

Valerie was accustomed to competition. As an undergraduate at Stanford University, she played on the Stanford women's tennis team. In her senior year in 1982 the Stanford University women's tennis team won its first NCAA national championship. She had also been a brilliant student at Stanford University but showed no trace of affectation. As an active member of the Stanford University Inter-Sorority Council, Valerie had been part of their governing body. The council organized social, educational and philanthropic events for all of the Stanford sorority women. It promoted excellence and encouraged high social and moral standards. Each of the seven individual sorority chapters promoted the four basic tenets that served to bind all the sorority members together. Those tenets revolved around scholarship, leadership, service and sisterhood. Valerie actively participated in each facet. She helped host dinner parties with professors, took a leadership position in promoting the acquisition of critical skill sets, participated in clothing drives and car washes to raise money for worthy charities and engaged in girls' nights out, coffee chats, and barbecues.

These were the core attributes and values that Valerie brought with her to the La Jolla based Robert Kaplan Investment Services firm in 1986. That was two years after she graduated from the Stanford School of Business. She remained steadfast in adhering to her principles of honesty, decency and integrity. She would not deviate from them.

Unfortunately, her rival Jason Gianelli eschewed none of her endearing qualities or principles when he also joined the firm in 1986. He devised and employed devious tactics in achieving his over-riding passion to rank number one in the Kaplan investment firm. By denigrating and criticizing Valerie's investment strategies and by providing higher investment returns than Valerie he had developed and maintained the largest client base in the company. His annual commissions far surpassed hers.

"You have an excellent investment record with our firm, Valerie," Kaplan said. "Yes, but it doesn't come close to matching Jason's record," she replied. "That may be true but his option strategies are risky," Robert said. Valerie suspected Jason's total accounts were significantly higher than hers, but that was a closely held secret. He certainly enjoyed an extravagant lifestyle. He was also saddled with a hefty monthly alimony payment to his former wife, Judy Gianelli. Their divorce five years earlier had been extremely contentious and well publicized. Judy had wisely hired one of the top divorce lawyers in southern California and it had paid off handsomely. She was awarded their beautiful La Jolla home overlooking the Pacific

Ocean and a generous monthly alimony check of $15,000 dollars. Jason could at least use the $180,000 per year alimony tax deduction, but it must have riled him to write out that alimony check each and every month. To rub it in even further, Judy had begged Valerie to manage her investment account. Judy knew that would grate upon Jason's psyche too. Knowing that Valerie was earning a commission on some of the money he was paying to her each month was bound to upset him.

Judy had just left Valerie's room. She had chatted enthusiastically about her new boyfriend, Richard Rizzo. It was somewhat ironic that Richard was a successful investment advisor with another prominent investment firm, one of Kaplan's chief competitors. Judy had even bragged over the fact that they were living together, but never intended to get married. Neither of them wanted to lose Jason's monthly alimony check.

Both Valerie and her husband, Charles were finally alone in her room. "So you couldn't find a way to sneak Sasha into my hospital room," Stephanie said. "What happened to your ingenuity, Charles?" she asked. Her face brightened up as she let out a laugh. "Well I can assure you Sasha wanted to come with me," Charles said. "She seemed heartbroken when I left her at home alone."

"Instead of enjoying Sasha I had to listen to Judy brag about her new boyfriend and how much they delighted in spending Jason's alimony check each month," Valerie said. "She may be beautiful, but she is certainly self centered and selfish. I imagine she shielded those qualities from Jason before they got married." "What precipitated their divorce?" Charles asked. "I think it had to do with Judy's refusal to have children. She had confided in me that children were a headache and expensive. She thought that they would interfere with her social life. Jason had pleaded with her to have children, but she refused his requests. That must have been a great disappointment for him," Valerie said. "Jason was a star football player at Notre Dame," Charles replied. "He must have yearned for a son, one that he could potentially groom into an athlete." "Yes, I'm sure he wanted at least one son," Valerie replied. "Any son of his would have great potential."

She had to admit that Jason possessed superior genes. Now they were just going to waste. He was smart, handsome and rugged. Women were naturally attracted to him. In fact, she thought, quite a few women would be happy to bear him a son.

Valerie was attractive but not beautiful. Her auburn hair and dark brown eyes complemented her appealing face. Her allure was based upon her shapely figure, engaging smile and pleasing personality. She had a crooked scar on her chin from a skateboarding accident that occurred when she was fourteen years old. It was a blemish but it wasn't disfiguring. Actually it was a distinguishing mark that people noticed but soon forgot.

For the past three years Jason had been dating Stephanie Shea, Valerie's closest friend and a major client. They were not as yet engaged to be married, but Stephanie had confessed to Valerie that she longed to be his wife. Stephanie had lost her much older husband to colon cancer five years earlier. She was still only 43 years old and very attractive. Besides that she was a generous and warm person. She was also rich. Her late husband had been a very successful entrepreneur in San Diego and had left her with a great deal of money when he died. He had been an investment client of Valerie's for the 10 years preceding his death. Before he died he had urged Stephanie to remain invested with Valerie. He appreciated her steady returns.

Jason was probably wary of women following his divorce from Judy. He would be suspicious of their motives in marrying him. Despite his alimony payments he had accumulated a sizable estate over the 24 years he was actively engaged in option trading with the Kaplan investment firm. Valerie thought marrying Jason would be a terrible mistake. She knew he had no scruples. But Stephanie described him as being wonderful to her and she loved him deeply. Valerie just didn't trust him. She thought trust was something every woman wanted and deserved in a marriage.

# Chapter 5

LATER THAT NIGHT Robert Kaplan returned near the end of the evening visiting hours. They were alone now. Robert had formed the Kaplan Investment Service 35 years earlier in La Jolla, California. He had enjoyed a very successful career as a Wall Street investment advisor in New York City. He decided to open his own firm. After exploring several cities on the west coast, he finally settled on La Jolla for his investment firm. Situated in a beautiful setting overlooking the Pacific Ocean, it was a destination site for the wealthy. The surrounding hillsides offered incredible home views and sound home values. He had gradually built up his business and now employed 16 investment advisors with Valerie and Jason being the best. He dangled the vice presidency of the company as a carrot in front of his employees. He knew both Valerie and Jason vied for the post. Whoever gained the position would be richly rewarded. Their investment commisson would increase to 0.0175. A paid membership up to $100,000 to a country club of their choice would go with the position along with a $25,000 per year car allowance. Vacation time would double to 6 weeks per year although he doubted that anyone who took the job would take off six weeks a year. He could be wrong. Both of his two leading candidates were making enough money to afford the time off. The biggest plum would be assuming the presidency after he retired. Of course he had no intention of retiring soon, but he was 68 years old. He might have to retire sometime in the future over health issues.

Jason wanted to become vice president of the firm. It was his contention that the investment advisor with the largest client base and the highest commission income deserved to be the vice president. He discounted the fact that his co-workers despised him. As vice president he might become generous and even teach them some of his current option strategies. In that position he would have more prestige and eventually he would take over the company when Robert Kaplan retired. Jason would also have more control over Valerie. What he failed to realize was the fact that Robert Kaplan was committed to honesty and integrity in dealing with clients and co-workers. They were qualities that Jason sorely lacked. Until Jason demonstrated those attributes his chances of becoming the vice president were remote.

"Valerie I have decided to grant you a two month leave of absence from the firm. That will give you enough time to recover," Robert said. "I don't think I'll need that much time off. I was thinking of returning to work within the next two to three weeks." she said. "I don't think that will be necessary. You can work from your home after each orthopedic rehab session. You can maintain contact with your clients by phone. They can even join you in your home for conferences," he said. Being absent from the office worried Valerie. She thought of the walk-in clients that would likely gravitate to other investment advisors including Jason in her absence. Jason would probably take advantage of her situation to hold additional mini seminars on option trading extolling his excellent returns and potentially luring more clients from her to him.

Robert read her mind. "Valerie, I think you can afford to take two months off from the office. If you miss some new clients, you can make it up when you return and are completely healthy. This is what I would really like to know. What are your long term goals with the company?" he asked. "Robert, you know that I yearn to ascend to the vice presidency of the company. I freely admit that the prestige and financial benefits of that position intrigue me. Other than that I want to become one of the top 100 women investment advisors in the entire USA. If I continue on my current account trajectory, I think I can reach that goal within the next six years," she said. "A third goal of mine is to become a knowledgeable investment mentor to the other investment advisors in our office. I want to evolve into becoming their respected investment educator, someone they can turn to for investment ideas and market timing. I know that will require spending more time studying and attending VectorVest seminars in order to know when to buy, what to buy and when to sell. I would like to help each of them grow their client base as I grow mine. If I can help them improve their clients' investment returns, they will in turn prosper through increasing their commissions. Finally I want to seek ways to modify my toxic relationship with Jason Gianelli. I recognize the fact that our competitive relationship is unhealthy and I would like to change it. I just don't know how to do it, but I include it as a long term goal." "Those are lofty goals and I applaud you for them," Robert said. "I hope you reach and attain each and every one of them. As you know, I've had a hard time deciding on who should become the vice president. That person will eventually become the president of the company when I retire. As president, you assume a great deal of responsibility which I am sure you appreciate. Right now I want to relieve you of stress and not create more. You are one of my most valued employees and also one of my closest friends. We attend the same synagogue and we mutually support some of our favorite charities. I admire your generosity." "Robert, I don't want people to think that I was promoted just because we are both of the same faith. I want to be promoted based upon merit and merit alone," she replied. "I think you have all the qualities I require to assume the leadership role in this company and eventually take it over," he said. "It would be an honor to lead your company after your retire. But you don't plan on retiring any time soon, do you?" she asked.

"Valerie, when I lost my wife, Marilyn to breast cancer last year I was devastated. I have very little to live for other than my company now," he said. "It was a tragedy losing Marilyn," Valerie replied. "She gave you so much pleasure." "There's no substitute for her," he said. "I really don't have any hobbies. My golf game is terrible and gives me little pleasure. I'm still in mourning over the loss of her. The office is my haven. I admit that going home to an empty house at night is depressing." "Losing Marilyn has been very hard on you. She was such a lovely woman and so deeply in love with you," Valerie said. He smiled over the memories. "We had so much fun together. She was a wonderful bridge partner. Her cooking skills were incredible and her parties were always filled with laughter and happiness." "Charles and I certainly enjoyed playing bridge with both of you and also tasting Marilyn's delicious creations. She was a great companion. How could you not miss her? You were inseparable." "Yes we were and it was wonderful," Robert said.

"Our vacations together were fabulous. I remember so well our trip to China sponsored through Oversees Adventure Travel out of Boston. We had read several books and articles about the dynamic changes occurring in China. We just had to travel to China together to witness those trends and changes," he said. "I remember how excited she was in planning that trip," Valerie said. "Where did you go first?" "We toured Shanghai and it absolutely astounded us. The gleaming new skyscrapers in the newly fashioned Pudong district belonged to many of the top fortune 500 global companies. The architecture was fabulous. One night we enjoyed a wonderful dinner in the revolving restaurant of the Oriental Pearl TV tower. From our table we looked down on the bustling cargo ships going up and down the Huangpu River laden with various products. For us Shanghai was a visible symbol of the new China's vitality and dynamism."

"After Shanghai, we flew to Beijing. There we strolled on a section of the Great Wall of China and toured the ancient Forbidden City," he said. "I remember the 1989 Chinese student protests in Tian'an Men Square that had such a gory climax," Valerie said. "Did you happen to visit that site?" "Yes we did. It's a vast open concrete expanse in the heart of Beijing. What is ironic in reference to the student protests is the fact that it is called the Square of Heavenly Peace. The way the Chinese police dealt with the student protestors was anything but peaceful," Robert said. "Chairman Mao Zedong's Mausoleum is also located there. They raise the embalmed body of Mao from his refrigerated chamber each morning and afternoon. We saw throngs of people lining up to view his body." "He died in 1976 Robert!" Valerie exclaimed. "We've done nothing like that in the United states. Yes, we have the Lincoln Memorial in Washington, D.C., but there is no refrigerated body of Abraham Lincoln." "Well I don't think we had the technology to embalm and refrigerate Abraham Lincoln when he was assassinated in 1865 Valerie!" Robert said. "I suppose not," she replied. Valerie's face lit up with a smile and she let out a laugh.

"I'm sorry I digressed. What was your next destination?" she asked. "From Beijing we took an overnight train to Xi'an. From there we took an air conditioned minibus to visit the excavated Terracotta Warriors guarding the tomb of an ancient tyrannical emperor named Qin Shi Huangdi. Pit one contained over 6000 warriors and pit two was filled with cavalry and more soldiers." "That's incredible. It must have taken decades to create all those soldiers," Valerie exclaimed. "We read that the emperor had enlisted 700,000 people over a span of 36 years in the tomb's construction. He also had 48 concubines and all the workers buried alive when he died." "What a terrible man!" Valerie exclaimed. "Hitler was much worse, Valerie!" Robert said. "He had nearly six million Jews killed during the Holocaust and another nearly 600,000 thousand Gypsies murdered. He was the most evil and hated man the world has ever known." "Hitler was despicable," Valerie replied. "I've also read stories about his masochistic concentration camp surgeon, Dr. Josef Mengele that were horrible too. His cruel work with gypsy children was particularly ghastly and chilling. I read where he would give sweets and toys to gypsy children and then lead them to the gas chamber. In one reported case he took a set of gypsy twins, Guido and Ina away. They were later returned to their parents in a horrible state. They had been sewn together, back to back, like Siamese twins. Their festering infected wounds were oozing pus. They would scream and cry continuously. Finally their parents killed them in order to end their suffering. Hitler's team contained a large number of contemptible sadists, Robert. But let's get off this sickening subject and return to your trip to China. Tell me more." "After being reminded of those regrettable historical events, it's hard to refocus," Robert said. "I know, but please try."

"Well we cruised the winding Yangzi River, visited Dali Lama's former quarters in Tibet and took the Peak Tram up to the top of Victoria Peak in Hong Kong before returning home. Sharing that trip with Marilyn was a special time in our lives together. We couldn't have done it after she developed breast cancer. You accompanied her on many of her trips to the hospital for radiation and chemotherapy treatments when the cancer spread to her bones. I appreciated your concern and devotion to Marilyn, Valerie." "We had a very special friendship, Charles. I wanted to spend time with her. I agonized over the bone pain she was experiencing. Despite her pain she often described her wonderful trips with you during our visits to the hospital. She had so many sacred memories of places you visited." "Well often people postpone taking exciting trips until it's too late," Robert said. "Thank God we didn't make that mistake."

Valerie watched as Robert's eyes began to glisten and she could feel his pain. She had observed in Robert his deep abiding love for his wife of 40 years. He was devastated by her premature death.

"You lost a very special companion," Valerie said. "I considered her to be one of my closest and most cherished friends. We both miss her." With that Robert started to weep and his whole body shook in grief. "I miss her so much. It's so hard to live without her." Valerie reached out to him and they hugged each other with a profound understanding. Robert could feel the depth and sensitivity of Valerie's compassion toward him. They shared their feelings of loss and they grieved together. Valerie could have just lost her life to a heart attack. She knew if that had happened Charles also would have been devastated.

At that moment she made a solemn vow to conquer her overt hostility toward Jason Gianelli. It was adversely affecting her health and her marriage. She didn't like it. Her reactions to Jason had to change.

# Chapter 6

DR. CREIGHTON, HER orthopedic surgeon, entered her room. "Valerie, Dr. Friedman has given me permission to start your right knee rehab program in three days. Do you think you'll be up to it?" "I think so," she replied. "It will be painful but I will provide you with a suitable analgesic to help control the pain. I will have you start slowly and advance based upon your tolerance. Dr. Friedman told me that your heart will stand virtually any degree of exercise. He said that the stent was placed so rapidly that you didn't sustain any heart damage. That's extremely encouraging. I want you back on the tennis courts within the next six months," he said. "I can hardly wait!" she exclaimed. "Tennis is the main activity that reduces my stress."

"By the way Valerie Dr. Friedman informed me that he intends to have you manage his investment portfolio," he said. "I hope that occurs," Valerie replied. "I would like to help him grow his assets. I owe him a great debt of gratitude for saving my life." "You were incredibly fortunate to have him here in the hospital when you had your heart attack," Dr. Creighton replied. "His technical abilities are amazing. Doctors come from all over the world to attend the interventional cardiology symposia he conducts."

"My investment portfolio is probably minor compared to his, but would you consider taking it over too?" Valerie was pleasantly surprised. It was the casual remark by her husband extolling her investment track record that was producing two new doctor clients. They were in the investor class that Jason vied for. They generated a high and steady income stream that usually far surpassed their spending. Frequently they suffered from poor investment results as they tried to manage their own accounts. They were usually too busy to explore the investment world for the best investments. Without training in the field they often made poor decisions.

Perhaps Jason appealed to some doctors who were able to tolerate more risk. Valerie knew that another group of doctors just wanted to preserve their capital and have it slowly grow. "I would be glad to be your investment advisor Dr. Creighton," she said. "I want you to know that I focus on generating a steady and safe return for my clients. I aim to not only preserve capital, but to have it grow mainly through the purchase of large diversified companies that grow their dividends through improving earnings year after year. Don't expect me to invest in risky assets because I abhor them. I don't buy call or put options. I do employ more conservative option strategies such as selling covered calls on stocks that we own or selling puts on stocks we would like to own but at a lower price. Do you think you would be comfortable with my approach to investing?" "Valerie I am much too busy to study and employ investment options. I tried to do it, but I just ended up losing money. I want to relieve myself completely from making investment decisions so I can focus on my orthopedic research and operations. It will be an incredible relief to turn it all over to you," he said.

Valerie had chosen Dr. Creighton based upon his credentials and his excellent results in performing total knee replacements. Total knee replacements had been used for a long time and the results in general were good. Most orthopedic surgeons didn't recommend playing tennis on hard courts after a knee replacement. Valerie knew of several nationally ranked senior tennis players with knee replacements. They were competing beautifully in national championships. A few, like Lenny Lindborg and Jim Nelson were even winning gold balls which were only given out to national champions!! She loved watching them compete with other notable senior champions such as Richard Doss and Bob Duesler.

"I want to compete in tennis at the national level again, Dr. Creighton" Valerie said. "Do you think that's possible with my right knee replacement?" "Yes, I think so" he replied. "Perhaps you should concentrate on doubles rather than singles. Your knee replacement will last much longer if you avoid excessive running and knee impaction especially on the surface of a hard court." At age 45 Valerie had reached the semifinals of both the grass and hard court national championships. Her right knee was already handicapping her then. She dreamed of entering the national 50 year old division next year. "I think I could limit myself to doubles," she said. "That would certainly extend your tennis career," he said.

The very thought of playing tennis again thrilled her. "I'm so grateful for what you've done for me. I will try to repay you by relieving you of investment decisions," she said. "That would give me a great deal of relief," he said. After Dr. Creighton carefully examined her knee, he excused himself and left her room.

Valerie looked out of the window from her hospital bed. Hang gliders were dipping and soaring over the Torrey Pines cliffs being propelled by up drafts. Golfers were swinging at tiny white balls on the Torrey Pines golf course below her. She had followed famous golfers on this same course just a few years earlier. She knew one of the best left handed professional golfers in the world lived in Rancho Santa Fe California only a few miles from the Torrey Pines Golf course. Although Valerie was an avid tennis player, she frequently attended professional and amateur golf tournaments with her golfer husband Charles. Golf was clearly one of America's favorite pastimes. The ideal San Diego weather made it possible to enjoy playing golf as well as tennis every month of the year. She would leave golf to her husband and his friends. It was too slow for her.

As the sun set over the Pacific Ocean, she reveled in the sight of beautiful shades of crimson red, purple and lavender. Soon she fell into a deep but troubled sleep filled with visions of a smiling Jason Gianelli.

# Chapter 7

AFTER SPENDING THREE days in a skilled nursing facility, Valerie returned home on June 17, 2010. She was controlling the pain in her right knee using an oral analgesic. She worked on bending and straightening her knee a little more each day. She also followed the specific exercise instructions provided by her physical therapist and increased her walking time daily. Fortunately, she didn't develop any signs of blood clots in her legs or infection in the operated knee. The hardest part for Valerie was not being able to drive her car for six weeks or to go into the office. She looked forward to returning to work, but resolved to stay out the office for the full two months recommended by Robert Kaplan.

It was a Saturday morning nine days later when her closest friend and favorite client, Stephanie Shea, entered Valerie's home for her two week investment review. Brady, her Bichon Frise blend was eagerly leading her into the room attached to his leash. Sasha, Valerie's Yorkshire terrier scampered into the room to greet Brady. The two dogs were great friends. Six years ago they had been adopted on the same day by Stephanie and Valerie from the Helen Woodward Animal Center in Rancho Santa Fe California. Both Stephanie and Valerie actively served as philanthropists in donating and raising funds for the center. They also actively participated in some of the center's sponsored events. One of their favorites was the dog surfing contest held each fall at Dog Beach in Del Mar California. In fact, normally after each investment meeting ended, Valerie and Stephanie would drive their two dogs together to Dog Beach. There they were released to romp and play on the sandy beach and shore of the Pacific Ocean. Dozens of dogs raced around sniffing and jumping. Some chased Frisbees showing incredible displays of athletic agility. It was pure havoc, but everyone and especially the dogs enjoyed the bedlam. Unfortunately today Valerie would not be able to participate in their ritual. Her total knee replacement prevented that from happening.

"I'm sorry I'm late Valerie. I just left Jason after a wonderful long walk and run at Dog's Beach with Brady. We had such a great time. I'm so glad Jason enjoys playing with Brady. They have so much fun together" "Dogs have a way of bringing people together," Valerie said. "Look how closely we interact with Brady and Sasha." "That's so true," Stephanie said.

"You should see how far Jason can sail a Frisbee. Brady is so fast he always seems to be able to run and catch it. Onlookers cheered and clapped when Brady made some incredible acrobatic leaps into the air to snatch the Frisbee. I think Jason and Brady have developed a very strong bond." Stephanie hoped that someday Jason would bond to her in marriage. That was her fervent hope. Then Brady would become an integral part of their family.

Valerie's heart was being torn apart listening to Stephanie rave about Jason. Stephanie was Valerie's best friend. Jason was her worst enemy. Brady and Sasha helped to bond Stephanie and Valerie together. No dog could bond Valerie to Jason. She detested him. He tried to dominate her as a money manager and lure her clients away from her. He was relentless in his pursuit of clients and that included those of all his co-workers in the Robert Kaplan firm. Brady loved both Jason and Valerie without any reservations. Unfortunately a wall of disdain separated Jason and Valerie. Stephanie was the potential bridge being loved by both of them. It especially distressed Stephanie to witness Valerie's profound dislike for the man she loved. She yearned to bring them together and to make them friends. But how? No solution entered her mind.

"Come right into my study Stephanie," Valerie said. "Would you like some coffee?" "I would love some coffee," Stephanie replied. "It's so nice of you to have me over again. How are you doing with your new knee?" "It's coming along just fine. The pain is subsiding and I'm getting around better every day. Besides I'm happy to report that your stock portfolio has just gone up by another one percent in the last three weeks!" "That's great. Maybe I can afford to buy some new clothes. Jason has invited me to a party at his home next month and I would love to show up in a new outfit," she said. Valerie blanched at the mention of Jason's name again, but quickly hid it from Stephanie's view. "What kind of party is he throwing?" she asked. "He says that he has invited a number of his clients and their wives over as a show of his appreciation for their business. He does this about once a month and says that it always pays off. Friends of his clients are regularly referred to him as a result of these parties," Stephanie replied. Valerie knew that Jason was very adept at generating new investment clients. He would probably extoll some successful option strategy during the course of the evening that generated a handsome return. "Well it's hard to match Jason's option trades," Valerie said. "I hope you are satisfied with the returns I create for you. Have you thought of switching your account to Jason?" "Valerie, when my late husband was dying he made me promise to stick with you. He was so grateful for the investment returns you had provided him over the years. He wanted a conservative approach to investing and not an aggressive style. He was very pleased with your steady returns. His main focus, he kept telling me, was to avoid the loss of capital. He wanted to preserve what we had first and foremost."

"You have been dating Jason for over three years now. Hasn't he asked you to turn over your account to him?" Valerie asked. "No, he's never even suggested that. I think he knows I am loyal to you. I know people recognize that I am rich because of the business success of my deceased husband. Jason has plenty of money and isn't dating me for my wealth. At least I hope that's true." Valerie suspected that Jason might harbor some devious thoughts in dating Stephanie, but she quickly dispelled them. "No Stephanie, I think Jason is dating you because he loves you rather than for financial reasons." Valerie thought to herself the fact that Stephanie was rich didn't hurt. Valerie knew Jason was a very materialistic man who focused more on financial gain than in creating friendships. His relationships with people were in general superficial. He didn't have a single friend among his co-workers.

"Let's sit down and review your latest investment results," she said.

Valerie had graduated from the Stanford School of Business in 1984. Upon graduation she had accompanied her roommate, Candice Christensen to La Jolla to visit Candice's parents. That trip changed Valerie's life forever. It was at a cocktail party at the home of Candice's parents that she met her future husband, Daniel Goldin, a post graduate computer engineer studying at the University of California San Diego. Robert Kaplan, the owner and founder of the Robert Kaplan Investment Service was also there. Two years later she was married to Daniel and working as an investment advisor in Robert Kaplan's firm.

"Stephanie, my major focus in selecting stocks is based upon identifying companies that have demonstrated a major percentage increase in their current and annual earnings per share. I have found that companies that increase their current earnings per share by 20 percent or more in the most recent quarter versus the same quarter in the year before generally have a superior rise in their stock price." "You have certainly picked some winning stocks for my portfolio," Stephanie said. "Since we are currently in a bull market, I am finding stocks that fulfill that criterion and they are doing quite well," Valerie replied. "You may recall in 2008 stocks fell rather precipitously. Earnings were dropping and I sold off the majority of the stocks in your portfolio." "I remember how far down stocks were falling in 2008. It was horrible," Stephanie replied. "Employing stop loss orders on your stocks resulted in only an 8% fall in your 2008 portfolio," Valerie said. "It was still a harrowing experience for me. Several of our bank shares fell right through my stop loss orders before they were sold. I anguished over the losses. There were investment advisors that lost as much as 50% of their client's money in that year. We're doing much better this year."

"Jason has told me he looks forward to bear markets. Why is that?" Stephanie asked. "Jason is an expert in selling stocks short and buying puts during bear markets. Sometimes he makes more money in a bear market than in a bull market. His clients did very well in 2008 because of his prowess in shorting stocks and employing put strategies. We had a down year. Several of my clients switched over to Jason in 2008. He was proud of that fact. Needless to say, it didn't please me." "I'm sorry that happened," Stephanie said. "I don't like it when you're hurt. You are much more than an investment advisor to me. You are my closest friend." Valerie's face lit up with a smile. It was so true. They were the best of friends.

"Let's forget about the stock market and enjoy some lunch," Valerie said. "I had some delicious pasta delivered to my house before you arrived to celebrate this occasion." "What occasion?" Stephanie asked. "I became independent of my crutches today. Now as you see I am only using a cane to get around!" "I guess that's true progress," Stephanie said. "You bet it is. It won't take me long get rid of this cane either." Valerie could not tolerate being an invalid.

# Chapter 8

AFTER LUNCH, STEPHANIE left and Valerie prepared for her next very important meeting to be held with Dr. Daniel Friedman, the cardiologist who had saved her life. She wanted to repay him by investing his assets wisely. She planned to do her utmost to obtain him as a client. She didn't know that Dr. Friedman had lost both of his parents in a terrible auto accident two years earlier. He had a very close relationship with them and was heartbroken. It was no surprise when he took a three month leave of absence from the La Jolla Clinic to grieve and help close out their substantial estate. He had inherited a great deal of money. Perhaps it was serendipity, but he was looking for an investment advisor to manage his assets when Valerie had her heart attack. They both stood to profit from their encounter.

Valerie had prepared her presentation when Dr. Friedman rang her doorbell. He was accompanied by his wife, Barbara and after she was introduced to Valerie they proceeded to her study. "Would you care for some coffee before we start?" Valerie asked. "No, thank you. We're just fine," they replied. "First, I would like you to know that the Robert Kaplan Investment Service has one of the lowest fee structures in the industry. On accounts under $1 million dollars we charge only 2.5% annually paid in quarterly installments. We charge 2.25% annually on accounts between $1 and $3 million dollars divided into quarterly payments. On accounts over $3 million dollars we only charge an annual fee of 2% again divided into quarterly payments. I don't know how much you plan to place with me, but you can see the fee schedule is quite reasonable." Dr. Friedman replied. "Valerie we will definitely be in the lowest fee structure." Valerie was both shocked and pleased. The Friedmans were wealthy and had planned on putting a great deal of money with her.

Valerie continued. "I am a very conservative investor. My goal is to provide my clients with an annualized return of 12% after fees. This has been my average annualized return over the past 24 years. Using the rule of 72 by dividing 12 into 72 my clients have been doubling their money every 6 years. I will try my utmost to maintain and perhaps even exceed that goal in the future. Of course I can't guarantee it. Do you have any questions?" she asked. "What criteria do you use in selecting stocks Valerie?" Dr. Friedman asked. "I pick safe and undervalued stocks that are rising in price," she replied. "That's a great idea, but how do you do it?" he asked. "I study a wide variety of investment newsletters and several newspapers. Besides certain newsletters I scout for investment ideas from various financial papers and services. Actually, the best source I use for my stock picks comes from using the trading software contained in VectorVest. It's a stock analysis and portfolio management system that was devised and founded by Dr. Bart DiLiddo, PhD. I began to subscribe to VectorVest in 1998 and it has proven to be the best investment I have ever made," she said. "It's really that helpful?" Dr. Friedman asked. "After I read Dr. DiLiddo's short ninety six page book entitled "Stocks, Strategies and Common Sense" that accompanied his CDs and literature, I was hooked. His treatise made the most sense of anything I had read or studied up to that point in time and even since then. I have used it faithfully and it has paid off handsomely. I tend to follow his prudent investor selections as I hate losing money," she said. "Do you buy speculative stocks Valerie?" Dr. Friedman asked. "As a rule, I don't invest in ultra conservative or speculative stocks. My goal is to both preserve and grow your net worth. Using VectorVest Prographics, its computer software program, I can enter my investment criteria and search for companies that meet them. For example if I want to find stocks that are extremely safe and have an attractive growth rate, I can enter those criteria into the VectorVest program and it will provide me with the names of companies that meet those criteria. I can add additional criteria and eventually find stocks that I think will be winners. Then I can follow those stocks and make adjustments in portfolios in order to meet my client's investment goals," she explained. "My investment returns have significantly exceeded 15% annually since I started using the VectorVest system." "It's really that helpful?" Dr. Friedman asked. "Absolutely," Valerie said. "The software gives me the ability to not only identify the general stock market direction, but it also provides me with insightful information about an individual stock's current relative worth, safety and timing. I use that information to choose the best stocks to buy. My goal as a prudent investor is to both pre-serve and grow your net worth. May I ask what goals you have in mind for your investments?"

Barbara was quick to respond. "We would be delighted with a 12% annualized return," she said. "We have tried to do our own investing and I'm afraid the results have been far less than yours. In fact last year we ended up losing money even though the general stock market was up in 2009." Dr. Friedman looked dismayed. "It was mainly my fault, Barbara, and not yours. You had opted for safe stocks and I gambled. I thought I could reap large gains on some biotech companies, but on several occasions I was wrong. The FDA approval didn't come through on two start up drug companies and they tanked. I wish I had known about you Valerie last year. We would be many hundreds of thousands of dollars ahead!" he said. "I'm so sorry!" Valerie replied. "I wish I had met you under different circum-stances too. But you saved my life Dr. Friedman and I will pledge to do my best to grow your portfolio."

"I do want you to know that I don't buy call options or puts. I may sell call options on stocks that we own or sell puts on stocks that I would like to own at a lower price. These are relatively conservative option maneuvers that can add to the growth of a portfolio. I don't short stocks either. The VectorVest program provides excellent opportunities to make money from stocks that are going down in price, especially during a confirmed bear mar-ket. I prefer to buy contra funds in a bear market. I admit that my invest-ment returns could have been significantly better in 2007 and 2008 if I had used VectorVest to short stocks falling in price and if I had employed better stock options." "Well, we lost a great deal of money in those two years," Dr. Friedman replied. "I doubt that we would have lost as much had our in-vestment account been with you during that period of time." "VectorVest is a very powerful stock analysis service," Valerie said. "I continue to study the strategies of the week, attend VectorVest seminars and our local user group. It's an ongoing educational process that is serving my clients well. VectorVest helps me remain flexible and to exercise the highest degree of investment prudence in selecting strategies to make money under changing market circumstances. I will do my best to use it wisely in making your investment portfolio grow in value over time."

The Friedmans were impressed by both Valerie and the VectorVest investment service. After exchanging a few pleasantries, they asked to be excused. "Valerie, Barbara and I will discuss the matter of assigning our account over to you over the weekend. May I call you tomorrow evening in case we have made our decision?" "Of course you can," Valerie replied. "We usually retire around 10 PM. If you call anytime before then, it will be fine." "Thank you very much for having us over to your lovely home. It has been a pleasure meeting you Valerie," Barbara Friedman said. Saying that, the Friedmans turned and left her home. Valerie looked out the window and saw them driving away in a beautiful teal blue Mercedes Benz. She could only wonder what amount of money they were considering to potentially place with her. They had indicated it would be over $3 million dollars. That would potentially become her largest account if it indeed occurred.

# Chapter 9

VALERIE HAD CHARLES drive her to the La Jolla Clinic for her cardiology appointment with Dr. Friedman. She was excited to see him. The Friedmans had turned their investment portfolio of $6 million dollars over to her during the week following their visit to her home. It was by far her largest account and she was ecstatic. She was ushered into an examining room by a nurse. Dr. Friedman entered the room and she greeted him with an enormous smile. "Before we start, Dr. Friedman, I want to thank you and your wife again for entrusting so much money with me. I will do my utmost to make it grow and grow safely," she said. "We know that Valerie. We had a long and in depth conversation with Robert Kaplan before we made our final decision. He affirmed your record with his firm and equally important to us he lauded your outstanding character. Mr. Kaplan has found you to be honest and upright in dealing with your clients. He told us that his wife had died of metastatic breast cancer last year and that you were one of her closest friends. He also informed us that you had taken off time from the office to be with her during her chemotherapy and radiation therapy sessions." "She needed support Dr. Friedman. She would have done the same thing for me," Valerie replied. "Well Robert Kaplan appreciated your concern for his wife. He said she was also very grateful for the emotional support you offered her. You were the only person in the office who seemed to care. He admires and trusts you Valerie. With that kind of endorsement we felt comfortable in putting our investment account in your hands. But now let's turn to your medical condition," he said.

"I have reviewed your lipid panel and only the moderately elevated LDL, the bad cholesterol of 135 is unacceptable to me. That level is too high and can contribute to coronary artery disease. Your HDL, the good cholesterol, is excellent at 80 and your triglycerides are normal. You have observed a healthy diet, have no signs of diabetes and have a normal blood pressure. You have a fine genetic history with both parents alive in their 70's. I discount the history of heart disease in two of your grandparents since they were both heavy cigarette smokers. Did you exercise regularly before your right knee became a problem?" he asked. "I have been an athlete all my life Dr. Friedman. I played competitive tennis at Stanford on the women's tennis team. Until the right knee stopped me I was working out at the gym three times a week. My schedule included some intense aerobic exercises."

"Well I am surprised by all of this. I think stress must be playing a significant role in your premature heart disease," Dr. Friedman said. "That could well be. I take my job very seriously and I monitor the stock and bond markets closely. I am constantly weighing a multitude of factors in my quest to make money for my clients," she replied. "Well stress does play an important role in inducing heart disease. Stress hormones like adrenalin are released during duress. Platelets become stickier, heart rate increases, blood pressure rises and even cholesterol can increase with stress. If a plaque in a coronary artery ruptures, the platelets tend to stick together forming an obstructing clot which leads to a heart attack," he said. "Is that what happened to me?" Valerie asked. "Yes, that's exactly what happened to you," he replied. "The total knee operation was an acutely stressful event, but there must have been other longer lasting stressful aspects involved in your life before that operation took place. Am I right?" he asked. "Yes, I suppose you're right," she replied. Valerie knew he was right. She experienced stress everyday in her office. Managing her accounts was stressful. Jason was even more stressful. "Well I'm not one to prescribe a tranquilizer," he said. "I wouldn't take it if you prescribed it for me," she said. "I will try to manage my stress in other ways."

Valerie had decided not to reveal her incessant battles with Jason Gianelli. Clearly Jason was the major stressor in her life. She was unaware that he was largely responsible for activating the flow of stress hormones into her system. Perhaps she would confess the rage that brewed inside her over Jason during a subsequent visit. She knew he represented a constant threat to her client base and was impeding her ability to reach the top 100 women investment advisors in the USA. Wasn't it understandable that she should harbor hostile feelings toward him? How was she to know that hostility could cause the release of inflammatory proteins into her blood stream which could potentiate coronary artery narrowing? Yes, she was frustrated and perhaps even mildly depressed. It was tragic that her coping skills were so impaired. She had no training in stress reduction techniques. In the meantime she would try her best not to let her anger toward Jason upset her life.

She would also be very careful not to reveal the fact that the Dr. and Mrs. Friedman had turned their sizable investment account over to her to manage. She knew Jason would try to convince them that he could better improve their investment returns. If he discovered the size of their account, he would try his best to take it away from her. Valerie decided to keep their account a secret. In fact she intended to call Robert Kaplan and ask him to help her do that as soon as her appointment ended.

"Well, Valerie, I'm going to prescribe a statin to help lower your LDL cholesterol. That should help reduce your future risk of coronary atherosclerosis. It's more expensive than some of the other lipid lowering agents," he said. "If you can't afford it, just let me know." She gave him a broad smile and laughed. "I know you say that in jest. With the commissions I will generate from your account alone, I think I'll be able to afford it," she replied. "I thought you would see it that way. We want to help each other, don't we?" "Well you saved my life and I will do my best to assure your financial well being."

With that Dr. Friedman left the room and Valerie prepared to leave too. She was ruminating over the stress Jason was causing in her life. Dr. Friedman had suspected stress was the major cause of her heart disease. Why hadn't she told him about Jason? Then again, what could he do about it?

Valerie called Robert Kaplan from her cell phone and when he answered she gave him a big "thank you!" "For what Valerie?" he asked. "You said so many nice things about me to Dr. Friedman and his wife."

"They were all true. I didn't have to lie. They deserve you," he replied. "You will give them the safety they desire."

"Robert I would like to ask a favor of you." "What is it?" he asked. "I would like you to keep their account with me a secret from all the other investment advisors and most of all from my nemesis, Jason Gianelli." "I will certainly do that for you. I don't think that Dr. and Mrs. Friedman would accept Jason's riskier approach to investing but of course I could be wrong," he said. "Well if he doesn't find out about it that risk is reduced, isn't it?" she asked. "That's a very reasonable assumption," Robert said.

"Well, I am keeping my pledge to you and will not reenter my office for the entire two months of sentencing you have imposed upon me are up." she said. Robert scoffed. "I have sentenced you to a well deserved vacation. You certainly don't take them on your own volition. I am sorry it took a total knee replacement and heart attack to make you take a relaxing rest."

Valerie was overjoyed by the fact that she had acquired the Friedman's account. It was clearly now the largest account in her client investment base. Then an annoying thought emerged. How could Jason steal the Friedman's account from her? Even though it was a secret she grew apprehensive. He had his devious ways to make things happen. But not in this case, she thought.

# Chapter 10

WHEN JASON LEARNED that Valerie would not be returning to the office for two months following her heart attack, he realized that he had been afforded a unique opportunity.

First he had to establish a friendship with the night office watchman. Jason brought a large pizza to the office at midnight to share with Vern Branch, a recently hired security guard. Three months ago Vern had left the US Army after serving one tour in Iraq and another in Afghanistan. Shrapnel was still embedded in his left shoulder. "Are you glad you're out of the service, Vern?" Jason asked. "I'm very glad" he replied. "My wife and our ten year old son missed me terribly. I missed them too. My mother in Scranton Pennsylvania constantly worried about me the entire time I was overseas. She disapproved of the wars I fought in."

They soon became friends. "I like to work late in the office when it's quiet and everyone's gone," Jason said. "I can get a lot accomplished." Vern was glad too. He appreciated the free food.

The next two nights they again shared midnight meals together. They were delicious and helped to further cement their relationship. Jason learned that Vern was barely getting by financially and that he wanted to buy his son a bicycle for his eleventh birthday. Jason pulled out his wallet and generously handed Vern a $100 bill. "This will help you buy that bike for your son," Jason said. Vern had never held a $100 bill in his hand in his entire life. He just stared at in gratitude. He could visualize the delight his son would have riding his first bike. "Thank you Mr. Gianelli," he said. "I don't know how I can repay you." "This isn't a loan Vern. It's a gift. You just re-payed me when your faced lit up with a smile."

Jason knew Vern would not scrutinize his late night activities. He had accomplished that goal so easily. Now he had to proceed with his mission.

Jason had carefully searched Valerie's office for her computer password but to no avail. Her filing cabinets and desk drawers were securely locked. He examined every post-it stuck onto the side of her computer tower. He identified addresses, user names and passwords for various investment letters and for tennisplayer.net, but could not find her computer password. There were several magnets originating from various places around the world attached to the metal sides of her computer tower. He pulled each one up and looked underneath for a hidden computer password. He became frustrated as he couldn't find it there or anywhere else in her office. She must simply have memorized it and placed it in her home safe, he thought. He would have to employ different methods to gain access to her computer files.

Jason purchased the exact model of Valerie's desktop computer and loaded it with her computer software program. In the privacy of his home he practiced computer hacking techniques that he learned from online sources and books. Secure in his knowledge and hacking ability he entered Valerie's office at one am early on a Monday morning and turned on her computer. After pressing the start button on her computer tower, he immediately held down the F8 key before the "Windows Starting" screen appeared. The Windows Advanced Option Menu appeared and he clicked on the Safe Mode with Command Prompt. Next he scrolled down to the bottom and selected "All Files." He typed in batch.bat and saved the file. He went to that site and opened it to obtain Command Prompt. Clicking on User/add he typed in C>netuserUsername/add. Then he added a new password and pressed enter. Using the new password he accessed and successfully downloaded Valerie's client master files including stock trades and actual banking transactions onto his own CD disk. Retreating to his office he placed the disk into his personal computer and studied her client accounts.

Jason was surprised to learn that a Dr. Daniel Friedman and his wife Barbara had recently given Valerie $6 million dollars to manage. The

Friedmans became Valerie' s largest account. He realized that Dr. Friedman must have been the cardiologist who saved Valerie's life. There was also a smaller recent account from a Dr. Creighton amounting to $400 thousand dollars. If these were her treating physicians, she had done well in securing their respective accounts, he thought.

He left his office at three am in the morning. At eleven am Jason called the La Jolla Clinic and asked if Dr. Friedman worked there. "Yes, he's one of our cardiologists," the operator said. "Please connect me to his office." Dr. Friedman's secretary answered and Jason identified himself as one of Valerie Goldin's office co-workers. "I understand Dr. Friedman recently saved Valerie's life after her heart attack and I would like to thank him," he said. "I will give him your message. He's terribly busy and probably won't be able to get back to you for one or two days." "That will be fine. I'm just grateful. Valerie is one of my closest friends."

Jason was proud of himself. He had become proficient in using sophisticated methods to cover his digital trail by deleting or bypassing electronic logs. Even if their office administrator detected an intrusion into Valerie's computer, he would not be able to to detect who had done it or what information had been viewed or downloaded. Jason had defeated the safeguards established to monitor and deter people from looking at Valerie's computer information without her permission

Jason was envious of Valerie's success in gaining these two accounts. He couldn't tolerate it. He felt compelled to develop a longer term plan to wrest the Friedman account away from Valerie. That would require a series of well orchestrated steps. He was adept at luring clients away from his co-workers. He had been successful in doing that on several occasions. Even some of Valerie's best clients had abandoned her for him. His co-workers might despise him for doing that to them, but he didn't care. He could easily rationalize his actions. After all, his outstanding returns were capable of luring clients into his stable. They were the best in the Kaplan Investment firm.

Besides that Jason was motivated by his desire to secure and maintain his mother's financial viability. He would never forget the abuse and suffering she had endured at the hands of her husband. When he lost his job he had left her nearly destitute. The generous monthly checks Jason was sending to her gave her financial independence. Her security and happiness gave him tremendous satisfaction.

# Chapter 11

DURING THE FIRST week Jason invited Dr. Friedman to play golf with him at his private golf club in La Jolla. During that first round Jason actively taught Dr. Friedman some of the finer aspects of golfing strokes including putting lessons. During later meetings he spent time informing Dr. Friedman about the leveraging advantages of option trading. Jason touted his 16.6% annualized rate of return over the preceding 24 years and forecasted a 30 percent or higher return in 2010. He could tell Dr. Friedman was impressed. Jason's goal was to convince Dr. Friedman and his wife to abandon Valerie as their investment counselor and to turn their money over to him to manage. He promised, but of course could not guarantee them, higher returns. Perhaps he could only gain part of their account from Valerie, but $6 million was a tidy sum to share with her. When Dr. and Mrs. Friedman accepted Jason's invitation to his cocktail and dinner party to be held on July 31, he was delighted. His invited clients would confirm Jason's superior investment returns compared to those Valerie produced over the years. Jason had purposefully invited some of Valerie's former clients knowing they would give their reasons for leaving her in favor of him.

The night before the party Jason had dinner with Stephanie and pre-pared her for the gathering. "Everything will be catered. You will be free to enjoy my guests," Jason said. "Dr. Friedman has informed me that his wife, Barbara loves her Labrador Retriever named Charity. Apparently he is such a gentle and content dog that Barbara has him involved in therapy sessions with autistic children." "Why is she involved with autistic children?" Stephanie asked. "Barbara's younger sister, Rebecca Cohen has an autistic son, Aaron, who is enrolled in a Carlsbad California school that caters to autistic children. Barbara has noticed that Aaron and many of the other autistic children react positively to Charity at the school."

Stephanie was intrigued. "I wonder if Brady could successfully engage in similar therapy sessions." "Why don't you ask her tomorrow night," Jason said. "I'll do that. I wonder just how successful her dog's interactions with autistic children can be? I would think it would be hard to measure the effects. I've read that human interactions with autistic children are often disappointing, but I've never personally encountered an autistic child. Have you?" she asked. "No I haven't. Dealing with Aaron has been difficult for Rebecca. According to Dr. Friedman she has experienced a great deal of frustration, disappointment and hurt in raising her son. Besides that Rebecca is challenged by her own battle with breast cancer." "Oh, my God. She has breast cancer too!" Stephanie exclaimed. "I can't imagine raising an autistic son and battling breast cancer at the same time. It must be a struggle."

"After Marilyn Kaplan developed breast cancer, Robert Kaplan and Valerie both began to support the Susan G. Komen organization," Stephanie said. "Their work in supporting breast cancer research and many additional aspects of breast cancer has been outstanding." "I've read that over 400,000 women a year die of breast cancer worldwide," Jason said. "Since breast cancer can run in families, Barbara has an increased risk of developing the disease too. She must be aware of that possibility and worry about it."

Stephanie was familiar with the devastating effects of metastatic cancer. Her husband had suffered during his four year battle with metastatic colon cancer. She had become depressed during and after his death. Every year she donated money to the Cancer Society.

"Jason you never mention donating money to charity. Have you thought about your role in serving those in need and giving back to your community some of your time, money and talents?" Stephanie inquired. "Yes, I do it by supporting catholic charities," he said. "I want to help individuals and families achieve self sufficiency and make a better life for themselves. I've dedicated my life toward making money for myself and my clients. I would be terrible at working in a day shelter trying to serve meals to the needy. By my donations to catholic charities I'm helping those who are struggling," he said. "How did you get started supporting these catholic charity agencies?" Stephanie asked. "I was moved to contribute when I witnessed their disaster relief efforts during Hurricane Katrina. I could only imagine how people were suffering from lack of food and water, the loss of their home, the crisis of not having critical child care and the lack of transportation." "Yes, we lead privileged lives living here in La Jolla," Stephanie said. "I can't picture myself involved in cleaning a mucked out home, removing debris, replacing furniture and appliances or helping to rebuild a badly damaged home," Jason said. "But I saw on television dedicated staff workers from various catholic charity agencies working every day after the storm hit doing what I couldn't imagine doing myself. That's why I committed some of my earnings in support of these agencies and I feel good about it."

Stephanie was pleasantly surprised. She was unaware of Jason's charitable contributions. He had kept it a secret. Perhaps he wasn't as unfeeling as most people judged him to be. Did his anonymous philanthropy serve as a means toward his personal redemption? He was certainly relentless in his pursuit of new investment clients and he seemed to delight when one of Valerie's clients defected and joined him. Stephanie thought Jason's charitable donations probably helped assuage his guilt in stealing clients away from his co-workers. She wondered if this was his way of compensating for his aggressive and selfish tactics. In his lack of goodwill and compassion toward his fellow investment advisors he was flawed. Were his charitable donations enough to compensate for his behavior? Certainly not in the eyes of Valerie. Stephanie could not be sure.

Still there was a modicum of Christian Charity that resided in Jason's soul and she embraced that side of his character. He did dedicate himself toward serving his client's financial needs, and he did deploy some of his earnings to charity. She wondered. Did these two factors serve to offset his egregious actions?

# Chapter 12

JASON WAS EXPLAINING his latest option strategy to Mr. Armstrong when he heard a loud exchange going on outside of his office. "Get Mr. Gianelli out here immediately or I will start to scream," Judy Gianelli shrieked. "I'm sorry but he is in a conference with a client and is not to be disturbed," his secretary responded. "I don't care who he is with. Just get him out here or I will barge into his office," she yelled. His secretary buzzed Jason and said. "Your former wife is out here and she is livid over something. Can you break away for a moment to talk to her?" she pleaded. Jason winced. She was the last person on earth he wanted to see. Jason entered the lobby from his office. Judy saw him and screamed. "Where is my alimony check? It's late. What am I supposed to live on?" Jason responded calmly. "I mailed the check to your home over two weeks ago." "Well I'm not living there Jason," she bellowed. "How am I supposed to know that?" "My attorney was supposed to notify you." "Well he didn't, so just go home and collect your check before I cancel it." "You wouldn't dare. I would have you back in court so fast your head would spin." "Why don't you marry the man you are living with?" Jason asked. "He makes a great living." "And lose your monthly alimony check! Why would I be foolish enough to do that?" Judy replied. "Just get out of this office Judy. Everyone can see what a bitch you are."

Some of Jason's fellow co-workers were smiling. They were glad to see Jason accosted. It didn't happen often enough they thought. "He's so smug and patronizing. I wish she had slapped him in the face." "Maybe he would slap her back. Then she could charge him with assault and battery." "Not if she struck him first," someone replied. "I didn't see it that way. Did you?" They all laughed.

"I often feel trapped by Jason. He's like a pirana attacking his prey and we are his victims." They turned and glared at Jason.

Jason noticed their anger and lashed out at them. "Get back to your desks," he shouted. "Put your feeble minds to work, and try to make some money for your clients. If you don't, more of them will leave you for me. I can outmaneuver the whole bunch of you and that isn't very hard."

Hate welled up in the minds and hearts of those listening to his barbs. "You are such an egotistical bastard," one of them said. "Your ethics stink. You may be smart in trading options, but your morals are in the gutter! Friendships mean nothing to you, Jason. Making money is your God. I hope when you die you will be alone and miserable."

Another co-worker said. "You in essence killed John Davenport, Jason." "I did not. He was a drunk and depressed," Jason said. "No, he hung himself because of you. You took away his clients and he committed suicide. He left a wife and two children destitute. We arranged and funded an office relief fund to help them out financially. Did you contribute to it? No, not a dime, but everyone else did. You didn't even have the decency to attend his funeral. You are a pathetic human being."

Jason only laughed. "All of you are jealous because of my success. Your puny investment returns will haunt you. I will pick up the pieces from your clients as they abandon you." He left them angry and frustrated. Only Valerie came close to matching his returns. They felt helpless knowing he was lurking in the background and eager to take away their clients.

"He's so smug and full of himself," a co-worker said. "I hope he suffers some disastrous trades this year. He needs to be put down several notches." They shrunk back to their desks. They knew their efforts to outclass Jason would be futile. He was just smarter and better trained than they were.

Jason returned to his office and Mr. Armstrong. "You were actually married to her?" Mr. Armstrong asked. "Yes, I was unfortunately. She was great for the first few years of our marriage. Then her true character emerged. It was horrible. She turned out to be the most selfish and self centered woman I have ever known. Before we were married she swore she wanted to have children. After we were married she stayed on the pill and refused to discontinue it. She claimed children were too expensive and would interfere with her social life. I finally had enough and divorced her," Jason said. "She's a real plum," Mr. Armstrong said. "I wonder if her boyfriend realizes what she's really like." "I doubt it," Jason replied. "She's pretty shrewd and hides her true character behind a mask of sweetness. But let's forget her and concentrate on my most recent option strategy for you."

"I subscribe to an option strategy service out of Chicago that's very powerful. The founders often appear on the TV business channel and they are brilliant," Jason said. "I have used many of their option strategies very successfully over the years. The current option strategy I'm using to enhance your investment portfolio is a call spread." "What does that entail?" Mr. Armstrong asked. "It involves the purchase of an in-the-money call option with an extended time horizon and the subsequent selling of out-of-the money, short duration calls." "That's a bit confusing to me," Mr. Armstrong said. "Let's see if I can clarify it for you," Jason said.

"In essence, the purchased call option becomes the foundation on which calls are sold against it. Option values are a function of the price of the stock, volatility and time. All options decay in value with time. The idea behind this strategy is to take in the premiums of the short term calls which are sold to help pay for the longer term call option that has been bought." "I think I need an example to understand it," Mr. Armstrong said. "I can do that for you," Jason replied. "On July 1, 2010 this company's computer shares were selling for around $260. I bought an October $255 strike price call for $16. That means the share price has to rise above $16 plus $255 or $271 per share before it expires on the third Friday of October 2010 for me to start making money on it. Since each call represents 100 shares, I paid $1600 plus commissions. Then I sold the monthly July $265 call for $6 and took in $600 in premium for 100 shares. If the share price of the company is under $265 by the third Friday in July, I pocket the entire $600. If the share price is rising above $265, I will buy it back before it expires and lose some of the $600 I was paid." "What if the share price falls to $250 in July 2010?" Mr. Armstrong asked. "Well I would still have collected $600 from the July option premium to help offset the $1600 I paid to buy the October call option. On paper I would be down $1600 minus $600 at the end of July, but I would have nearly three months for the share price to recover before the October call I purchased expires. In the meantime I can sequentially sell the August, then September and then October monthly call options to potentially gain another $1800 in option premiums which more that cover the original $1600 I spent to buy the October 255 call option. Does that make sense?" "I'm afraid I'll have to better digest what you've just explained to understand it," Mr. Armstrong said. "What do you hope will happen to maximize my profits on this call spread strategy?" he asked. "I want the share share price to slowly rise, so I can take in most of the option premiums I sell each month. Then in October I want the share price to rise above $271. I will then sell the $255 call option I bought for $1600. Let's say I sell my call option on October 14, 2010 when it reaches $280. The intrinsic value of the option would be $280-$255 or $25. The option value remaining might be $3, making the total worth $28 times 100 or $2800. Adding this to the $2400 in sold option premiums means I would make $5200 on a $1600 orginal investment!" "You mean to tell me that I would gain $3600 on a $1600 investment," Mr. Armstrong said. "That's right," Jason replied. "So you would more than double my money in under four months if everything goes right," Mr. Armstrong said. "That's exactly right. It might not double, but I think the gain will be significant. We are in a bull market and the shares are rising. I admit it's a bullish call option spread on a hot technology stock. I have my own money heavily weighted into this option play, Mr. Armstrong. I think we'll be happy with the results come the end of October 2010." In fact Jason had purchased 100 $255 call option contracts for $160,000 in his personal account. He was that confident it would pay off.

Mr. Armstrong would become ecstatic later in the year. On October 15, 2010 Jason sold his $255 call options for his clients and for himself. He sold the calls when the share price reached $315 on that date. The intrinsic value of each option was $315-$255 or $60. Multiplied be 100 shares per option came out to $6000 per call option. There was $2 dollars of option value left when he sold the option for another $200. In addition there was $2000 of option premiums he had collected selling four monthly call options from July to October 2010. The total amounted to $8200! Subtracting the $1600 cost of each option left a profit of $6600! Jason had purchased on the average 5 call options for his clients, but 100 for himself. He was the big winner amassing a profit of $660,000! It would be the largest profitable option play of his career. He would indeed have a stellar investment return for his clients and especially for himself in 2010.

"I'm glad you're investing my money, Jason. I barely understand these option trades. Even if I understood them I couldn't handle the stress involved in following them." "That's why you have me managing your account. I monitor these trades daily and I can exit a losing position quickly if I find the trade is going sour," he said.

"You have certainly made my account grow, and I appreciate that." "Well you have shown your appreciation by referring some of your friends to me. I have been making them money too. I am throwing a cocktail and dinner party at my home in four weeks on July 31, 2010. It's on a Saturday night. I would welcome the chance to meet some more of your friends and share some of my investment thoughts with them. Your invitation is in the mail. Just mention their names on your RSVP and tell them they are welcome to join you. There will be plenty of catered food and I will be offering some outstanding wines from my cellar." "My wife and I will definitely attend and I will take the opportunity to invite some of my friends. I can let you know their names and addresses in case you want to send them a personal invitation," he said. "That's a great idea. I will mention your name on the invitation. Then when I start making money for them it will reflect well on you. After all, that's what friends are for."

Mr. Armstrong recalled that Jason had made him a great deal of money in 2008. Several of his friends had lost up to 50% of their portfolio in that same year. Yes, he thought, Jason was a genius when it pertained to investments. He certainly failed when he married Judy Gianelli though. She had put on a real display of hostility in the office today.

# Chapter 13

JASON INTRODUCED STEPHANIE to Dr. Daniel
Friedman and his wife Barbara at the onset of his party. He left Stephanie
with Barbara and took Dr. Friedman with him to meet some of his investment clients. Jason beamed as clients raved about their 2010 investment
gains. "Your option trades are doing brilliantly," Mr. Armstrong said. "I'm
waiting for the housing market to rebound" Jason replied. "We should have
some spectacular gains from our option trades on the home builders when
that occurs." Dr. Friedman realized that Jason was a talented investment
advisor just as he was as an expert in invasive cardiology. He was learning
that Jason was a standout in option trading. He inwardly chastised himself
for not employing an investment specialist earlier in his career. He had lost
a great deal of money by thinking he could be superior to experts in managing his personal investments. At least he had placed their investment
portfolio with Valerie who had an outstanding and consistent performance
record. Should they consider Jason in managing a portion of their portfolio?
He was without a doubt impressive and his record was exemplary. His
clients were certainly pleased with their investment returns.

Stephanie was actively engaged in conversing with Barbara Friedman
over their mutual love of dogs. It turned out that Barbara's Labrador
Retriever, Charity was also taking surfing lessons in preparation for the
September 8th, 2010 surfing contest to be held at Dog Beach in Del Mar.
Stephanie also learned that they had a mutual investment advisor, Valerie
Goldin. "Barbara, Valerie is my best friend. She has a wonderful Yorkie

named Sasha who is also taking Saturday surfing lessons along with me and Brady. Why don't we all get together and enjoy the surf with our dogs?" "That's a great idea and then we can have lunch together at my house afterwards. Would you like to do that?" Barbara asked. "That sounds appealing to me. Let me run it by Valerie."

Only those who love dogs realize what a strong bond dog lovers can have with each other. "Charity is such a content and calm dog that I have him interacting with autistic children," Barbara said. "Autistic children tend to live in their own private world often wordless and remote. My older sister Rebecca has a 14 year old autistic son named Aaron. She often feels hopeless and discouraged in dealing with him. Charity seems to help Aaron escape from his private sanctuary, even if it's only momentarily. That's what has motivated me to share Charity with other autistic children. I've witnessed Charity's positive effects on Aaron." "Your sister must be grateful," Stephanie said. "The look of appreciation on Rebecca's face has often moved me to tears. I would do anything to help lift Rebecca's spirits," Barbara said. Stephanie could only imagine the profound gratitude the two sisters had toward Charity and the love they had for each other. "You have a very special dog in Charity, Barbara. I hope he will like Brady and Sasha." "I'm sure he will," Barbara said.

They could hardly wait to test the meeting of the three dogs during surfing lessons at Dog Beach.

Stephanie could feel Barbara's warmth and compassion. She already liked her and looked forward to becoming her friend. She imagined their dogs would help secure their friendship. Dogs have a way of doing that.

At the dinner table the subject of investment returns dominated the conversations. Stephanie told Barbara Friedman how pleased she was with the investment returns Valerie Goldin was providing her. Mr. Armstrong overheard her remark and rudely interrupted. "Jason will easily surpass Valerie's returns this year as he has in the past. I switched from Valerie to Jason in mid 2007 when I found myself losing money with Valerie. Jason's returns exploded my assets to the upside during the rest of 2007 and during all of 2008. I kept a small portion of my account with Valerie for comparison purposes and I've witnessed the sharp discrepancies in their side to side results. Valerie's account was losing me money while Jason was giving me excellent gains." "This year I will probably double Valerie's returns," Jason said. "She may make 15 percent in 2010 because we are in a bull market. I'm on my way to making over 30 percent for my clients through my option strategies. That means for every $1 million dollars I will outperform Valerie by $150,000 dollars. When a bear market develops I will really excel. I know when and how to short stocks and buy put options. She doesn't. That's why so many of her clients have left her to invest with me in order to achieve higher returns." He looked so triumphant as he bragged about his investment prowess. Stephanie experienced a tinge of anger as she listened to Jason downgrade her best friend. He was blatantly attacking Valerie in front of the Friedmans who had entrusted their account to Valerie. It was an obvious ploy to gain their account and Stephanie felt helpless in defending Valerie. She didn't understand options and couldn't refute Jason's statements. She just felt his allegations were unfair and she was ashamed of Jason's actions. No wonder Valerie disliked and distrusted Jason. He did criticize her behind her back. She noticed the Friedmans were attentive to the remarks of Mr. Armstrong and Jason. "Aren't your option strategies riskier than Valerie's more conservative investment techniques?" Dr. Friedman asked. "Not at all," Jason remarked. "I hedge my option investments and use sophisticated methods to determine when to buy and sell my positions. I rarely lose more than 5 percent on any option trade. My upside gains on the other hand have exceeded 100 percent on several occasions. Valerie can't come close to matching my option profits."

Stephanie had to admit he was very convincing. She wouldn't change her account with Valerie, but she surmised the Friedmans might. She now understood why Valerie both feared and disliked Jason. He used these parties to disparage her and to gain more clients. She vowed to remain loyal to Valerie and hoped the Friedmans would too.

When the party ended she asked Jason to take her home. Tonight she wasn't proud of him.

# Chapter 14

THE FOLLOWING SATURDAY morning Barbara Friedman joined Stephanie and Valerie for their weekly dog's surfing lessons at Dog Beach. The Dog Surf A Thon contest was scheduled for Sept 8. Their dogs only had one more month to practice surfing. They laughed together watching the comical actions of their three dogs as they were being launched onto surfboards by their surfing instructors. Were these three grown women being ridiculous playing in the surf with their dogs? Probably, but they didn't care. They found clowning around in the surf with with their dogs to be hilarious. It was a beautiful sunny day, the water was warm, and they were having fun together. That's what mattered. They didn't want the morning to end.

Around noon they drove to Barbara's beautiful home in Rancho Santa Fe to have lunch together. There they were joined by Rebecca Cohen, Barbara's sister and her autistic son, Aaron. Valerie and Stephanie were fascinated watching Aaron's reactions to Brady, Sasha, and Charity as he sat mute in a corner of the family room. Barbara's gentle and caring labrador retriever, Charity was Aaron's friend and he reached out to pet him. He accepted Charity into his private world. Aaron appeared anxious and frightened when Brady and Sasha dashed over to his side. Stephanie and Valerie called back their two dogs and Aaron appeared relieved. It was so hard to understand and penetrate the workings of Aaron's autistic brain. They began to appreciate Rebecca's challenges in dealing with him on a daily basis.

During the course of their luncheon together the subject of Rebecca's battle with breast cancer came up for discussion. She related how she had missed her annual mammogram due to an extended business trip to New York City early last year with her husband. Eight months later she discovered a lump in her right breast. "I was diagnosed with stage three breast cancer," Rebecca said. "That led to a right mastectomy followed by eight chemotherapy treatments. Now I'm in the first month of three months of radiation therapy."

"You must have been frightened when you first discovered the breast lump," Stephanie said. "I was terrified," Rebecca said. "I was totally ignorant when it came to understanding breast cancer. My doctor advised me to carefully explore the Susan G. Komen website for more information about breast cancer. He wanted me to become better informed. It was only after I spent several hours studying their website that I better understood the disease and its ramifications." "How did you start your search?" Valerie asked. "First, when I opened up the website I clicked on the section entitled Understanding Breast Cancer. There I was able to access several areas of interest. Just reviewing the Understanding Breast Cancer Guide gave me invaluable insights into the disease. For example even though our family doesn't have any first degree relatives with breast cancer, I decided to have genetic testing done for the BRCA1 and BRCA2 genes which are associated with a higher risk for breast cancer. Fortunately they were negative. I'm currently enrolled in a San Diego Komen funded breast cancer support group. I've met some wonderful people and we give each other emotional support. I've learned we share one worrisome thought in common." "What's that?" Valerie asked. "It's the lingering fear that the breast cancer has already spread to other parts of our bodies. It just hasn't shown up yet. That's a gnawing, aching concern that seems to emerge daily. We hate it."

Stephanie's face registered concern. "I'll have to check out the Susan G. Komen website myself," she said. "Two years ago I had a negative breast biopsy after my annual mammogram discovered something suspicious. It was a very worrisome experience. I want to learn more about the disease."

"One of my best friends, Marilyn Kaplan died of stage four metastatic breast cancer last year," Valerie said. "We attended many of her chemotherapy and radiation therapy sessions together. We were such close friends. I've agonized over her death. Marilyn also attended a Komen funded breast cancer support group and she said it was very helpful. I've taken the opportunity to make a recurring donation in memory of Marilyn to the Susan G. Komen organization. They sent a tribute card to Marilyn's husband. He called to thank me and we recounted so many fond memories of times we spent together."

"We also support the Susan G. Komen organization, Valerie," Barbara said. "My husband, Daniel has been actively involved in cardiology research for many years. When he read about the annual Brinker Award for Scientific Distinction he was impressed. The Brinker Award recognizes and honors leading scientists whose breast cancer research and treatment efforts have advanced the Komen battle to save the lives of those burdened with breast cancer. Their research efforts have had and continue to have a significant impact on breast cancer."

It was such a beautiful day. As they finished eating, Barbara asked, "Would you like to go out to the patio and play some bridge?" "That's a great idea," Valerie replied. Both Stephanie and Rebecca agreed. Each of them loved to play bridge. The three of them had enjoyed being together at Dog's Beach in the morning. Now in the afternoon sharing Rebecca's dream of becoming breast cancer free and supporting Aaron had drawn all four of them closer. They were fast becoming friends.

They each had their own different personal dreams and goals. In their hearts and minds they each hoped to realize them. Perhaps with time that would happen. In the meantime playing bridge together became the more immediate challenge.

# Chapter 15

IT WAS A beautiful Saturday afternoon and two months had elapsed following Valerie's heart attack on June 12, 2010. Welcome Back Valerie balloons were floating around the main office room of the Robert Kaplan Investment Service. All of the investment advisors except for Jason Gianelli were mingling around the office chatting with one another and drinking punch. Some were munching on Hors d'oeuvres. They were waiting for Valerie's grand entrance scheduled for 3 PM. When Valerie entered the office cheers erupted. "Welcome back Valerie," they all shouted. Everyone was smiling. Valerie was very popular and deservedly so. She had mentored so many of those present over the years in the techniques, principles and strategies involved in making sound investment decisions. She had shown them how to generate income and stock price appreciation for their clients. They were deeply indebted to her. Jason Gianelli would not give them current option strategies. He held option seminars but they only alluded to trades done in the distant past. They were not necessarily relevant to current conditions. What was worse is the way he would steal clients from fellow advisors. During his option discussions he would announce his spectacular record of returning 16.6% annually to his clients. Then he had the audacity to ask if any of the participants were doing better than that with their current advisors. Of course no one in the office could match his record and that often caused clients to shift their accounts to him. That had occurred with almost everyone in the office including Valerie. They were happy Jason had not joined them to celebrate Valerie's return. They knew he was in his office with a client as they were partying. Making money ruled his life. He had no friends at this party.

Robert Kaplan stepped up to Valerie and announced: "Valerie this represents a present for you from everyone in this room." He handed her a heavy, beautifully gift wrapped box. Valerie opened it carefully and pulled out an elegant crystal vase. She cradled it carefully. Then Valerie lifted the vase high over her head mimicking the recent winner of the 2010 Wimbledon women's tennis trophy. Then like Rafael Nadal, the outstanding Spanish tennis champion who had just won back to back victories in the French Open and Wimbledon, she pretended to bite into the vase. Several people took her picture. She was warm all over. These were her friends. She genuinely liked them and she knew they appreciated and liked her. Handing the vase to her husband Valerie proceeded to thank each person in the room individually. Robert Kaplan beamed. He was so happy to have her return and she seemed to be very healthy. Picking up his glass Robert said. "I propose a toast. Valerie, we offer this toast to your good health and prosperity over the coming years. We wish you all the success in your career as one of the best investment advisors in the country." With that all the glasses were raised and a chorus of "hear, hears" filled the room.

It was after the applause ended that Valerie was stunned. The man coming out of Jason's office was her cardiologist and largest client Dr. Daniel Friedman. Dr. Friedman scurried toward Valerie and took her hands in his. "Congratulations on returning to your office Valerie," he said. "I can see everyone seems pleased over your return." "What are you doing here Dr. Friedman?" Valerie asked with a hint of dismay. She had noticed Jason retreating into his office and closing his door. "I have just concluded an investment meeting with your cohort, Jason Gianelli. He has described his warm relationship with you. During your absence Barbara and I have had the pleasure of meeting Jason and reviewing his investment returns. They are very impressive and we have decided to split our account between you and Jason. This provides us with an excellent conservative return from you and a higher though more speculative return through Jason's stellar option strategies," he said. Valerie was shocked. Her face grimaced in disbelief. "How did you come in contact with Mr. Gianelli?" she asked. "He actually called my office to thank me for saving your life. I thought it was a very fine

gesture," he said. "He didn't suggest a meeting to discuss his option investment strategies?" she asked. "No, he didn't. He did invite me to play a
round of golf with him the following Saturday which is my day off. I had
always wanted to play his country club course in La Jolla and when he
mentioned that's where we would play I was delighted," he replied. "Did he
bring up investing ideas during your round of golf?" Valerie asked. "No,
but he did give me some excellent golfing tips. My approach shots, chip
shots and putting have all improved due to his terrific instructions. You see,
Valerie, I am under such incredible pressure during the week in the hospital
that I find golf is the most soothing way for me to relax on my day off. But
please return to your welcome back party. Enjoy your friends. They are here
to celebrate your return." "Well, I have an appointment with you in two
days, this coming Monday. Can we continue this conversation then?"
Valerie asked. "Of course we can. I will look forward to seeing you." With
that he turned and shook hands with Charles and Robert Kaplan who had
sidled up during their conversation. A look of alarm was present on Robert
Kaplan's face as he watched Dr. Friedman leave the office.

"Did you hear what Dr. Friedman just said Charles?" she asked.
Robert Kaplan was also beside her now. "He's going to transfer $3 million
dollars from his account with me to Jason," she said. "Jason's despicable,"
Charles said. "How did he persuade Dr. and Mrs. Friedman to do that?"
His brows furrowed and his eyes narrowed in anger. He stomped on the
floor with his foot. He found Jason's actions reprehensible. Someday he
would confront Jason, but not today. He wiped away Valerie's tears and
hugged her tightly. "Why haven't the Friedmans informed you of their decision earlier Valerie?" "The transfer papers were probably just signed in
Jason's office this afternoon," Valerie said. "Jason referred to me as a cohort and implied I was his friend. I would like to strangle him." Robert
Kaplan was also dismayed. He was shielding Valerie's grief from the rest of
the crowd. "Robert, you and I were the only ones from our office who
knew the Friedmans had implemented an account with me. You were
sworn to secrecy," she said. "I've maintained that secrecy," Robert said. "I
never met Dr. Friedman in this office and only once in our home," Valerie
said. "Robert you personally delivered the client documents for him to sign
directly to his office. Jason didn't call Dr. Friedman right after my heart

attack. He called him at least a week after the papers were signed." "And I retained those papers in my office safe Valerie," Robert said. "Well the $6 million dollars was transferred to my account almost immediately after the papers were signed and I started investing it from my home computer. Somehow Jason learned that I had an account with the Friedmans and I don't know how he discovered that fact. Do either of you have any ideas?" she asked. "While you were out of the office could Jason have somehow gained access to your office computer?" Charles asked. "Your home computer is linked to it, isn't it?" "Yes it's linked, but he would have to know my computer password and that's locked up in our home safe," Valerie said. "No I think he would try to hack into your office computer at night when no one is here," Charles said. "Well he would still have to know my password," Valerie said. "Could he possibly guess it?" Robert asked. "It's made up of two higher and two lower case letters and 6 digits. The chances of deciphering that are remote," Valerie said.

"Well I'm going to set up a meeting with Dr. Friedman to discuss this matter further," Robert said. "I will do my best to ferret out the sequence Jason employed to win over one half of their account. Now please, Valerie, attempt to be cheerful and rejoin your friends. They've missed you and are eager to talk to you." Valerie sighed. She was so disappointed. "I'll put on a happy face but it will be a false one. I'm finding it very hard to stifle my anger toward Jason."

When the party ended, Charles and Valerie left the office and returned to their home carrying the beautiful vase. They had not noticed Jason furtively sneak out of the office while Valerie's back was turned. Some of the guests saw him leave but no one acknowledged him. Today he had been the office ghost.

# Chapter 16

VALERIE ARRIVED AT Dr. Friedman's waiting room the following Monday and was ushered into an examining room by his nurse. She was about to record Valerie's vital signs when Dr. Friedman entered the room. "I will check her pulse and blood pressure," he said and with that he excused her. "Valerie I had no idea that there was so much animosity between you and Mr. Gianelli. I thought you were cohorts working together to improve your clients' investment results," he said. "No, Dr. Friedman, we are actually rather intense rivals. We have our own distinct methods of dealing with our clients' accounts. Jason and I are poles apart in the way we manage money," she said. "I'm so upset over the fact that I caused you so much distress during your official welcoming back party," he said. "It wasn't your fault. Jason had convinced you to split your account with me. He's very artful and successful in the methods he employs to accomplish client transfers. I get so upset and frustrated each time it happens," she said.

Dr. Friedman noticed that her fingers were trembling and her face showed signs of distress. "Do your fingers tremble like this frequently?" he asked. "No only when I'm upset," she replied. Taking her pulse, Dr. Friedman looked up in alarm. "Valerie your pulse rate is over 150 beats per minute and it's grossly irregular. You're showing signs of atrial fibrillation." He ordered a stat EKG. The rhythm strip confirmed the diagnosis of atrial fibrillation. "I'm going to start an intravenous line and administer a medicine called diltiazem in an attempt to slow down your heart rate," he said. After the intravenous line was started, he returned with a vial of diltiazem and drew up 10 mg. He slowly injected it into the IV line over three minutes. As the fluid dripped into her vein, her heart rate slowly began to drop. "Haven't you noticed some funny sensations in your chest lately, Valerie?" he asked. "I did in the parking lot before we entered the La Jolla Clinic today. I had begun to relive the Jason situation and I noticed a kind of fluttering in my chest. I thought it revolved around my impending visit with you and our potential discussion over your account with me. I envisioned you and Barbara turning all of your money over to Jason and that alarmed me," she said. "We won't do that Valerie. In fact Barbara and I are very concerned over the way Jason has dealt with us. We can see now that he had developed a plan consisting of a series of meetings with us in order to gain a portion of our account. If we conclude that he deliberately set out to wrest our account away from you, we will dismiss him and return all of our assets to you to manage. We cannot tolerate duplicity in any form," he said. Valerie was relieved to hear that and her opinion of the Friedmans was reaffirmed. They were honorable people. They expected honesty in their dealings with people and they objected to hidden agendas. Valerie felt that they would uncover a deliberate and devious plan well orchestrated by Jason to land their account. She felt a tinge of hope.

After the initial bolus dose of IV diltiazem, Dr. Friedman had started a continuous infusion of the drug. It was exerting its effect and her heart rate continued to fall. She was feeling much better. Dr. Friedman excused himself to attend to other patients. He left his nurse to monitor her blood pressure and heart rhythm. "I'll be in the next door examining room and will check on you between patients," he said. He asked the nurse to notify him if Valerie's blood pressure dropped below 100 or if any other problems arose. Valerie chatted with the nurse in attendance. She remembered her husband, Charles, was in the waiting room. He was probably worried since over two hours had elapsed. "Would it be all right for my husband to join us?" she asked the nurse. "That would be fine. I'll go to the waiting room and bring him back," she said. Charles appeared and looked concerned when he saw her attached to an intravenous line. "What is going on Valerie?" he asked. "I developed an abnormal heart rhythm called atrial fibrillation. It's probably the result of stewing over Jason and his devious ways. He has a way of overwhelming me," she said. "But Dr. Friedman is going to review Jason's actions with Robert Kaplan after he finishes in the hospital this Wednesday and then later on with Jason. He said he would reinstate his entire account to me if he finds Jason had been devious in his dealings with him," she said. "That's great news," Charles replied. "But how serious is this atrial fibrillation you're experiencing?" "I don't know. I haven't asked Dr. Friedman that question yet. He'll be back soon and we can find out then."

When asked about the significance of atrial fibrillation Dr. Friedman gave them some startling news. "The major concern that I have surrounding atrial fibrillation is that it can sometimes lead to a stroke," he said. "A stroke!" Valerie exclaimed. "That would be the worst thing that could happen to me. I've seen people paralyzed on one side of their body after a stroke. Sometimes people can't even speak following a stroke and if they can their speech is garbled." "Valerie, we employ a blood thinner called an anticoagulant to reduce the chances of a stroke when someone develops atrial fibrillation," he said. "A stroke doesn't usually occur early in the course of acute atrial fibrillation anyway. I'll order an echocardiogram to look at the structure of your heart valves and chambers. In listening to your heart I haven't detected any heart murmurs. I really think that acute stress precipitated this event and hopefully we can convert your rhythm back to normal quickly."

Indeed that's exactly what happened one hour later. Her rhythm returned to normal. "Now that you're heart rhythm is normal I won't have to give you a blood thinner," he said. "I'll continue to monitor your rhythm over the next few hours to make sure atrial fibrillation doesn't recur before I dismiss you from the clinic today. I'll arrange to have you wear a Holter heart rhythm monitor for several days. Using the Holter heart monitor I can check your rhythm under various conditions and correlate it with what you were doing at that time. I'll count on you to record and time your various activities. In your case entering the time of any stressful events will be very important," he said. "Today confirms what I've been thinking since our last visit. Other than your moderately elevated LDL cholesterol you have no risk factors for premature heart disease other than stress. Your most recent blood studies demonstrated that the statin that I asked you to take is working beautifully. Your LDL cholesterol has fallen from 135 to only 68 in one month! That's wonderful. As to your stress, I'm going to refer you to one of the cardiologists in the La Jolla Center for Integrative Medicine. I simply dealt with an acute obstruction in one of your coronary arteries and unblocked and stented it. There's much more to the heart than physical obstructions," he said. "Stress is playing a major role in causing your heart disease. It clearly precipitated your bout of atrial fibrillation today. You need to learn techniques to help you control the adverse effects of stress in your life. Please immerse yourself in their programs. They'll help you in more ways than I can." "Does that mean I'm losing you as my cardiologist?" Valerie asked. "No, not at all. I will continue to carefully follow your course. We work together as a team."

Dr. Friedman taught Valerie and Charles how to take her pulse. "If you pulse rate exceeds 100 beats per minute and is irregular you need to call me or go to our urgent care clinic. That would potentially signal the return of atrial fibrillation and would require acute treatment again," he said. Later in the day Dr. Friedman checked her heart and rhythm one more time. He was satisfied that her normal rhythm had been reestablished. He discontinued the IV and handed her a scheduling slip.

She was to set up a revisit with him in one week and schedule an appointment to see a cardiologist in the La Jolla Center for Integrative Medicine. After thanking him, Valerie and Charles headed for the scheduling desk. Before leaving the clinic she was connected to a Holter Monitor and an echocardiogram was scheduled along with her two cardiology appointments.

Leaving the clinic Valerie expressed her deep appreciation of Dr. Friedman. "He's much more than an invasive cardiologist Charles. He's a warm and compassionate man. He truly cares about people and their problems. I'm more than just a temporarily blocked coronary artery to him. I can feel his compassion and empathy. Those qualities are important to me and are totally lacking in Jason Gianelli." "Let's forget Jason," Charles said. "Let's drive north down the Torrey Pines road past the ocean into Del Mar. I want to treat you to dinner and a drink at one of the ocean front restaurants. You more than deserve it. After your bout of atrial fibrillation, you can use some down time."

Valerie was petting Sasha who had vaulted into her lap when she first sat down in the front seat of their Lexus. Sasha's love for Valerie was unconditional and genuine. As she gently stroked Sasha's back, a warm blanket of calm settled over her mind and body. Her heart beat slowed even more. The connection between anxiety, hostility and her heart was so obvious she thought. Her reactions to Jason were so detrimental. He could have caused her to have a stroke today with her bout of atrial fibrillation. She realized that joining the La Jolla California Center for Integrative Medicine would be imperative. Learning methods and techniques to ward off and control Jason induced stress were absolutely necessary. A stroke would destroy her life. It had to be avoided.

"Before we go to the restaurant let's stop at Dog Beach and let Sasha enjoy some freedom. She could use a run on the beach," Valerie said. Charles agreed. "We could use some fresh air too," he said. As they walked happily hand in hand down the beach, they knew how fortunate they were to have each other. They enjoyed the ocean breeze and even the barking dogs. There would be much more chatter and noise at the restaurant, but they would enjoy the meal and drinks together. Valerie looked into Charles eyes and said. "I love you." Valerie knew she had a very special husband. She also knew he was worried. Perhaps the people and programs associated with the La Jolla California Center for Integrative Medicine would help her. It was certainly worth exploring that possibility.

# Chapter 17

THE NEXT DAY following her bout of atrial fibrillation, Valerie returned to the Robert Kaplan Investment firm to resume her job. After settling into her office, she turned on her computer to review her clients' accounts. The stocks she had selected for the Friedman's account were rising in value. She wondered what Jason would do with his half of the Friedman's money. Just thinking about it made her fume. She knocked on Robert Kaplan's door and was invited into his office. "Welcome back Valerie. Everyone has missed you!" he said. "I'll bet Jason didn't miss me. He was busy trying to steal my clients while I was recovering from my knee operation and heart attack scare. Robert did you tell Jason about Dr. Friedman's account with me?" "Of course not. We promised each other to keep that a secret," he said. "Then how did Jason find out about it?" she asked. "I have no idea. Why don't you go ask him?" "I'll do that," she said and she walked briskly out of his office.

Valerie charged into Jason's office without knocking. He was with a client and looked shocked when he saw her. "What do you think you're doing barging into my office like this," he shouted. "Get out of my office. I'm with a client." "I don't care if you're with the Pope, you thief," she yelled. Turning to his client she said, "I suggest you leave the room. This isn't going to be pleasant." The client looked puzzled and alarmed. He wasn't sure what to do. "Just sit where you are Mr. Murphy. She has no jurisdiction over you," Jason said. "Fine," Valerie said. "Hear this out. How did you find out Dr. Friedman was a client of mine Jason?" she shouted.

That caught his attention. "Mr. Murphy please wait in the lobby. This conversation shouldn't last very long." Mr. Murphy hurried out of Jason's office noting the rage on Valerie's face as he passed her. "No one in this office other than Robert Kaplan knew Dr. Friedman had become my client. He didn't tell you so how did you obtain that information?" she asked. She had a menacing look on her face. "I heard someone in the office who had visited you in the hospital mention his name," he said. "You're a liar. I was placed into the ICU coronary care unit after Dr. Friedman performed the balloon angioplasty and stenting procedure. No one other than my husband Charles was allowed to visit me. Think again Jason," she bellowed. "When were you discharged from the ICU?" he asked. "I was transferred the following morning. Why does that matter?" she asked. "Well some office members must have visited you and found out Dr. Friedman had operated on you," he said. "No, Jason, that didn't happen. Dr. Friedman visited me early in the morning before visiting hours. I didn't tell anyone the name of my cardiologist! Try again, Jason. How did you really find out?" Jason was nervous. He obviously couldn't tell Valerie he had accessed her office computer files illegally late one evening while everyone was gone. "I may have called the nursing station to inquire about your status. A nurse may have mentioned Dr. Friedman's name," he said. "You're pathetic, Jason. That would be privileged information. The nurses wouldn't give out his name. In fact Dr. Friedman told me that you called him three weeks after my discharge from the hospital. Isn't that a bit strange?" she asked. "It wasn't strange. I just wanted to thank him for saving your life," Jason said. "No, Jason. You wanted to steal his account away from me. That's why you called him, isn't it?" "Of course not," he said. "Then why did you suddenly invite him to play golf and then meet with him on several occasions while I was still out of the office?" she asked. "I was just being friendly," he said. "You aren't friendly. You don't have a friend in this entire office. The only time you feign friendship is when you have an ulterior motive. In this case you had somehow found out that Dr. and Mrs. Friedman had set up an account with me and you wanted it. Isn't that the truth Jason?" she said. "Get out of my office Valerie. I don't like your false allegations. You're just mad because the Friedmans turned half of their account with you over to me to manage. They won't be satisfied with your average returns. They know I can make them more money," he said. "The only way they would know that is because you touted your returns to them. You probably planted some of your bragging clients around the Friedmans at your dinner party. You're so clever Jason. But most of all you are an unethical thief. I hate you Jason. I hope you rot in hell!" She turned and left his office slamming the door. As she passed by Mr. Murphy she said. "You can go back in now. I am through with that bastard."

Several co-workers cheered as Valerie left Jason's office. They couldn't help but overhear the shouting and accusations that went on in his office. "You sure reamed him out, Valerie," one of them said. "Yes, but it did me no good. I still don't know how he found out about the Friedman's account with me." None of her co-workers could help her unravel that mystery. "We didn't know you had an account with him either," they said. "Somehow he found out and took away half of the proceeds in my account," she said. Scowls crossed the faces of several co-workers. They were angry too. "He probably hired someone to hack into your computer while you were out of the office, Valerie. He can't be trusted. He'll do anything to gain clients. That would include hacking into computers and lying."

He is so formidable Valerie thought. How can I successfully compete with someone who is so smart and unethical? She couldn't prove he stole the Friedman's account or any of her other client's accounts. It was so frustrating and stressful. She hoped she could cope, but it was becoming hard.

Yes, she had ignored Dr. Friedman's advice to remain calm, but she was furious. Jason has violated every investment advisors' code of ethics. You don't steal client accounts. Jason had his own set of rules and they were despicable. She was glad Dr. Friedman had shown her how to take her pulse. She wasn't surprised when it was 105 beats per minute. Fortunately it was still regular. Even after her tirade atrial fibrillation had not returned. She knew more emotional outbursts like the one she just experienced blasting Jason could provoke atrial fibrillation. She shuddered over the thought. She could potentially have a stroke. Her next step was to carefully record the time of her encounter with Jason on her Holter Monitor diary card. She speculated that the peak heart rate would have probably occurred at the height of their conflict. The results of their meeting were disappointing. Jason had somehow secured the information regarding her account with the Friedmans. How he did it remained a mystery.

She briefly thought that he probably did hack into her computer, but her computer password was locked in their home safe. She knew nothing about computer hacking techniques. Could they do it without a password? She doubted that was possible. Just the same she thought she had better change it. She realized she had not changed it in over a year.

Jason resumed his conversation with Mr. Murphy. He had been referred to Jason by Mr. Armstrong. It was ironic, he thought. Jason had carefully seated the Armstrongs next to the Friedmans during the client dinner he had held at his home. He knew the Armstrongs would brag about the excellent returns Jason was producing for them. That was probably the night he had hooked the Friedman's account.

The encounter with Valerie had left Mr. Murphy nervous. He said that he would have to talk with his wife some more before placing money with Jason. Now it was Jasons turn to be angry. "Don't let the ranting of a jealous co-worker rattle you Mr. Murphy," he said. "She can't match my returns and gets very upset when one of her clients turns money over to me to manage." That didn't convince Mr. Murphy and he left. I'll get even with you for this Valerie. Yes, he thought, I will find a way to get even with you.

# Chapter 18

ROBERT KAPLAN CALLED Jason into his office on Thursday, the day after he had met with Dr. Friedman over dinner. Robert had been assessed of all the Friedman's encounters with Jason over the preceding five weeks. He now had a clear understanding of the methods Jason had employed to gain half of their investment account with his firm. It was time to get Jason's version of the story. Jason entered Robert's office and greeted him with a degree of suspicion. "What's this meeting about Robert?" he asked. "Jason I understand you are going to manage $3 million dollars of the Friedman's account. Is that right?" he asked. "Yes, they have turned over that amount to me," he said. "How did you manage to do that Jason?" Robert asked. Jason was visibly nervous. "I invited him to attend one of my option classes and he liked what I presented," he replied. "But how did you get to know Dr. Friedman in the first place?" Robert asked. "I found out that he was the cardiologist who saved Valerie's life from some of the people in the office. I called Dr. Friedman to thank him for doing that," Jason said. "Then after just one option class with you he turned over $3 million dollars to you? Isn't that a bit farfetched Jason?" he said. "What else did you do to land his account?" "I also invited him to a luncheon at the La Jolla Tennis Club to discuss option strategies," he said. "On only one occasion?" Robert asked. "Yes, only once," he said. "Did you have any other meetings with him?" Robert asked. "Yes, I invited him to a dinner party at my house and he came with his wife Barbara," he said. "Who else attended that party Jason?" he asked. "Just a few of my friends," Jason replied.

"When you say friends Jason were any of them client friends?" he asked. "Yes, I suppose some of them were clients," Jason said. "Did you bring up the subject of option trading to enhance investment returns at that dinner party?" Robert asked. "During the course of the evening a few of my clients mentioned that I had made a great deal of money for them using my option and short selling techniques," Jason replied. "So in other words Jason you courted the Friedmans on several occasions hoping to land at least some of their investment dollars. Is that right?" he asked. "Well I found him especially interested in my methods of creating excellent annualized returns. He found my option trading techniques to be fascinating. He is a very bright man and picked up on the leveraging advantages of options quickly," he said. "But all the while you knew that the Friedmans had an account with Valerie, didn't you?" he asked. "They both mentioned that to me during the dinner party, but they didn't reveal the size of the account Valerie was managing," Jason said.

"I have to confess that I too have interviewed Dr. Friedman," Robert said. "He informed me that he met with you on five different occasions during the past five weeks. The first time was a round of golf at your country club. He told me that nothing about investments was discussed during that golfing debut. He was grateful for the golfing instructions you gave him. But the next four meetings were all centered on your option and shorting strategies. You asked him specifically to let you manage his investment dollars. He also said you portrayed yourself as Valerie's friend. That was after he mentioned she was managing their account. Is that right?" Robert asked. "Well I didn't actually say a friend. I used the term cohort in describing Valerie," he replied. "But you implied she was a friend. That's the connotation Dr. Friedman derived from your description of your relationship with Valerie. You told him that you admired Valerie's investment prowess, but he said you also described it as stodgy and rather old fashioned. You said Valerie only sold covered call and put options. You termed those option strategies as plebeian and unsophisticated. Is that true Jason?" he asked. "Well I believe that those kinds of option trades fail to make greater returns. I can generate a significantly higher return with my techniques and my track record attests to that fact," he said. "But you also implied that Valerie would not mind sharing their account with you Jason.

Valerie is not your friend and never has been. Obviously she would lose $45,000 dollars a year in commissions on the $3 million they reassigned to you. Don't you think that would upset her? That's especially true since you have taken several other accounts away from her. She has been devastated by your actions. In fact Dr. Friedman told me she developed an acute heart rhythm disturbance this past Monday. That was just two days after her office party. It was the kind of rhythm disturbance that can lead to a stroke. He told me that stress was most likely the cause of this arrhythmia and I am accusing you of being the cause of her stress. She was so upset when she saw you emerge from your office with Dr. Friedman last Saturday that it ruined the rest of her day Jason. Valerie has been devastated by your blatant actions to steal her largest client. If she develops a stroke over this, I will never forgive you."

Jason shifted his feet uncomfortably in front of Robert. His face showed signs of dismay. "I didn't intentionally try to harm Valerie"' Jason said. It was immediately perceived as a brazen lie by the discerning mind of Robert Kaplan.

"Both Dr. Friedman and his wife are very distressed over your actions Jason. They will be in touch with you shortly. I told him that I had scheduled a meeting with you after my meeting with him yesterday. I offered to report back to him the gist of our discussion. In the mean time I suggest you apologize to Valerie and consider withdrawing yourself from the Friedman's account." "But I will make them much more money than Valerie," Jason said. "That may be true, but you employed deceptive actions in gaining their account. I am personally ashamed of you. You have humiliated me and this firm. In fact if you want to leave the firm, I will endorse it. Do I make myself clear Jason?" he said. "Robert I make this firm much more money than the top ten investment advisors combined. Do you really want me to leave?" he replied. "Jason I think you are a genius at what you do. There's no one in this firm that can match your returns. I just wish you would be honest in your dealings with our clients and stop trying to steal accounts from your co-workers. Do you want every investment advisor in this company to distrust and despise you? Do you think money is the only thing this company stands for? If you do, you're mistaken. I believe in honesty and integrity. You haven't shown either of these traits in dealing with Valerie and the Friedmans."

"If you want me to vacate this firm, I will consider doing so," Jason replied. "But I will take my clients with me." "You had better carefully review your contract with this firm. It clearly states that if an investment advisor leaves or is fired for misconduct, their client investment accounts stay with this firm for the following two years," Robert said. Jason was shocked. He always thought he could take his accounts with him if he left the firm. Losing his major source of income outside of his own investments for two years would impact him terribly. He would still have the $15,000 monthly alimony check to pay and that would certainly hurt. He could ask the judge for a review of the payment size, but he knew that could take a year or more. Judy's lawyers were shrewd and they could employ delaying techniques. In that case he would have to vacate some of his personal option trades to meet his monthly cash flow obligations. Jason hastily retreated from his threat to leave. "Robert I like working in your firm. I don't want to leave," he said. "Then I would suggest you mend some of your ways," Robert said. "You are excused. Please leave my office."

Jason wasn't surprised when Dr. Friedman called and scheduled a meeting with him the following Saturday. During the meeting in Jason's office Dr. Friedman reviewed their various meetings and Jason's relationship with Valerie. "From your conversations with me I thought you painted a strong and positive relationship with Valerie Goldin. I have learned that in fact the opposite is true. You have been combatants in the Robert Kaplan Investment Service for years. Valerie has a strong disliking of you and also distrusts you. You have taken several of her clients away from her by promising higher returns. Is that right?" he asked. "Clients have left her because I do generate higher returns," Jason replied. "But you schemed to get our account. In fact our account with Valerie had remained a secret according to Robert Kaplan. How did you find out about it?" he asked. "I didn't know about your account with Valerie," he lied. "I just called to thank you for saving her life." "You called three weeks later Jason? I find that hard to believe now that I know more about your relationship with Valerie. You courted me very actively. Somehow you must have learned about our decision to make Valerie our investment advisor. Barbara and I are impressed with your investment returns, but we are suspicious of your actions. We don't like deceit and duplicity. We suspect you have shown both in this matter. Consequently we've decided to withdraw our $3 million dollars from you and give it back to Valerie to manage," he said. "But I will make you more money Dr. Friedman," Jason said. "That may be true, but honesty and integrity mean more to us than just making more money. We can rest comfortably with Valerie's returns of 12 percent per year. We respect her moral values. They mean a great deal to us. Thank you for meeting with me Jason. I will expect to have our assets with you transferred back to Valerie this coming Monday. Do I make myself clear?" he said. "Yes sir," Jason replied. With that Dr. Friedman turned and left his office.

Jason was surprised by this sudden reversal. He thought that he had carried out his plan to get the Friedman's account brilliantly. He realized that meeting Dr. Friedman during the afternoon of Valerie's office return party had been a mistake. He vowed to be more careful the next time. With a devious smile he thought to himself. Your accounts are still not safe Valerie.

When Robert Kaplan informed Valerie by phone of Dr. and Mrs. Friedman's decision to transfer $3 million dollars from Jason back to her she was thrilled. "Why did they do that Robert?" she asked. "I think they realized that Jason had been manipulative and devious in wresting part of their assets away from you. They are very honorable people Valerie. I applaud them for their action," he said. "I will certainly thank them," Valerie said. "Dr. Friedman knew that stress had played a role in my acute bout of atrial fibrillation. After our conversation at my office return party and in his office, he knew that Jason and I were enemies and not friends. He has referred me to the La Jolla Center for Integrative Medicine. He said I will learn techniques on how to better deal with my anger and hostility toward Jason from experts in the center. I certainly haven't handled my hostility toward Jason very well," she said. "No, you haven't. I have sensed a great deal of underlying stress in your life," he replied. "I've had no way of measuring it. Perhaps you will learn various techniques to modify stress at this center." "Well I hope it doesn't revolve around weekly visits to a psychiatrist's couch. I don't want to spend hours discussing my childhood and my sexual fantasies," she replied. Robert laughed. "Do you think that's all they focus on?" he asked. "Well I've heard stories about three to four years of psychiatric therapy with only minimal results," she said. "Let's see what the program entails," he said. "Please let me know more about it once you've explored it in more detail." "I promise to do that."

Would the La Jolla Center for Integrative Medicine be helpful in controlling her hostility toward Jason? What techniques would she learn to effectively deal with the emotional turmoil he was creating in her life? Her curiosity was aroused. She would be grateful for any insights the center could provide her. Better than that would be the actual acquisition of methods to control her anger toward Jason. She became excited just thinking about it.

She could hardly wait to get started. Her reactions to Jason had become disabling. Hopefully the center would afford her opportunities and solutions to regain better emotional stability. Besides that anything that would help relieve her heart from the adverse effects of stress would be welcomed. She would embrace any techniques that would help thwart the future development of another heart attack or the onset of a stroke.

# Chapter 19

EXCEPT FOR THE reprimand by Robert Kaplan and the loss of the Friedman account the summer of 2010 was going beautifully for Jason. His option strategies were providing excellent returns. 2010 was shaping up to be a banner year. He was also taking time to actually enjoy the San Diego summer with Stephanie. They attended several fabulous musical concerts on Shelter Island together. Many of the dinner shows featured major singers, musical groups and other artists. The nights were balmy and the food delicious. It was a great way to enjoy outstanding food and music.

Savoring delicious food at some of San Diego's excellent restaurants also stood high on their list of pleasures. One of their favorites, Bertrand at Mr. A's was a famous restaurant known for its delicious cuisine and majestic views. From their table they watched the air traffic flowing in an out of Lindbergh Field. The view over beautiful downtown San Diego City out to the San Diego Bay was stunning. They enjoyed the view of sailboats wafting in the bay being moved by warm summer breezes. They also appreciated the appetizing food prepared by the renown Chef Martin Woesle and the music played by the celebrated Randy Beecher on the piano at Mille Fleurs, Bertrand's companion restaurant in Rancho Santa Fe.

La Jolla also hosted a number of excellent restaurants. One of their favorites was one located just above the Pacific Ocean. They found ordering specialty appetizers such as halibut ceviche and grilled octopus to be especially delicious. On another occasion as they crossed the curving Coronado Bridge on their way to the famous Hotel del Coronado for dinner,

Stephanie gazed down in wonderment on the myriads of sailboats moving across the San Diego Bay. She also noticed a huge aircraft carrier moored alongshore North Island, a symbol of San Diego's strong military presence. "What an incredible view Jason," she said. "This has to be one of the most beautiful bridges in the entire United States." "I agree," he said, "but I wouldn't want to commute over it every day going to and from work. I imagine the morning and early evening traffic is pretty heavy."

After a delicious seafood dinner, they meandered to the dance floor. They loved to dance together. Jason was such a superb dancer despite his slight limp. Stephanie noticed women glancing at him with admiration. She was happy that he was with her. She imagined that many of the women on the dance floor would have gladly exchanged their partners in order to be dancing with Jason.

Life during that summer was certainly treating them well. On another night they relished a delicious meal at The Prado at Balboa Park restaurant. Following their dinner they entered the Old Globe Theater across the street. There they thoroughly enjoyed the lively Shakespearian play "The Taming of the Shrew." Yes, there was so much to see and do in San Diego. It was an ideal place to live.

Since his option trades were flying high, Jason thought he would surprise Stephanie by offering to take her on a vacation for one week. "You plan it Jason. I'll go anywhere with you," she said. Jason looked forward to an escape from his office and wanted to show Stephanie how much he loved her. He hoped to create a more deepening intimacy with her. He thought a splendid vacation would serve to further ignite their passion for one another and he eagerly planned it. Her birthday on September 12, 2010 provided the added impetus and opportunity for such a vacation celebration.

He carefully arranged a romantic trip to idyllic Napa Valley in northern California. It was August 31, 2010 when he put on his Armani cologne, a light blue blazer, and matching blue slacks to take her to a romantic restaurant in La Jolla for happy hour, dinner and dancing. In that setting with the ocean waves breaking below them he told her of his plans for their vacation. Stephanie was excited. "Jason it will be wonderful spending a week with you in Napa Valley. When are we leaving?" "On September 11th, the day before your birthday. I want to celebrate your birthday sipping the best Cabernet Sauvignon I can find. In doing my research for this trip I learned that Napa Valley has continued to be one of only nine great wine capitals in the world. Besides that it was voted one of the world's finest food and wine destinations. There are more Michelin restaurant stars, 14 to be exact, in the Napa Valley than any other wine region in the world on a per capita basis," he said. "It sounds fabulous, Jason. I can hardly wait to go with you. I'll take this opportunity to go shopping for some new outfits and shoes." Jason thought that women looked for any excuse to buy clothes, but in this special case, it was fully justified. "You just go out and do that. Surprise me with your selections."

Before leaving on their Napa Valley trip Stephanie shared an important dog surfing contest with Valerie on September 8. It was the annual Helen Woodward Dog Surf a Thon contest held on Dog Beach in Del Mar. The event attracted dogs from all around the country. It raised thousands of dollars in support of orphaned dogs looking for forever families as well as other important canine projects. Brady, Sasha and Chariity had a surfing advantage because it was their "home beach." Stephanie, Valerie, and Barbara had arranged and paid for professional surfing lessons for their dogs on the weekends in July and August. Of the three dogs Brady was doing the best on his surfboard and was a definite contender to place in his weight division. There was a Jack Russell Terrier who had won the tournament in 2009. He was incredible on his surfboard and was the favorite to repeat as the overall winner in 2010.

On the day of the event over 4000 spectators mingled around Dog Beach enjoying the sun, the beach, and the surfing and doggy costume competitions. They cheered the dog surfing contestants rooting for their favorites. Everyone seemed to be having a great time. The Beach Bum Costume contest was hilarious. The owners displayed their rich imaginations in creating the colorful, zany and wild looking dog costumes. Photographers were everywhere. Videos of all the surfing action were memorializing the event. Valerie was especially pleased over the overwhelming financial success of the fundraiser. She had pledged $1000 to sponsor Sasha. Stephanie and Barbara had done the same in support of Brady and Charity. Their donations would help support the variety of Helen

Woodward Animal Center projects. Valerie personally served as a volunteer in their Pet Encounter Therapy program. In that role she enjoyed the visits to senior centers, youth facilities and hospice patients aimed at promoting the love of animals. There she witnessed the positive effects dogs engendered in their interactions with people. Yes, she thought dogs do have a very special place in society.

Even though Brady, Sasha and Charity failed to win the surfing contest in their respective weight classes, they did well. The three owners had every right to be proud of their dogs. In addition to having fun together they were delighted by the overall success of the event! Splashing together in the surf with their dogs brought the three of them closer. They had become wonderful and happy friends.

Beside musical venues, delicious meals, dancing and plays, Stephanie and Jason found time to play golf on the weekends. Each Sunday morning Stephanie attended church at Horizon in Rancho Santa Fe. She found the pastor to be inspirational as he followed biblical scripture passages during the church service. She was also attending a women's home bible fellowship program sponsored by the church. She had joined the group soon after her husband died. The group had provided her with deep emotional support following his death and it continued to be an integral part of her life. Someday she hoped Jason would establish a stronger relationship with the Lord and accept Him as his savior. She doubted that would ever happen. Jason was not a spiritual man. His catholic church attendance was irregular. On the other hand he was generous in his support of catholic charities and for that Stephanie was thankful. His financial success was at least partially serving some worthy charitable causes. In truth rather than attending parish church services Jason preferred to spend his time playing golf. At least he was willing to start his golf game on Sunday afternoons. By doing that Stephanie could play along with him following the end of her church ser-vice. That was a concession she appreciated.

Jason was an incredible scratch golfer. Once Stephanie asked. "Have you ever considered a career as a professional golfer?" "No, I haven't" he replied. "It would be challenging, but I wouldn't want to spend that much time travelling around the country. I'm very happy living in La Jolla and figuring out winning option trades. They're very stimulating and when they are successful my clients are pleased and so am I. The stock market is rising so my call options are doing quite well. Golf is just a pleasant pastime. We'll be able to play golf together in Napa Valley, Stephanie. The resort I've booked has two splendid golf courses."

Stephanie was excited over the impending trip to Napa Valley. She had never been there, but had heard from friends that it was a beautiful place to visit.

# Chapter 20

STEPHANIE WAS EXCITED and called Valerie to tell her about her impending trip to Napa Valley with Jason. She wondered if Valerie and Charles would allow Brady to stay with them during their Napa trip. "We would be delighted to have Brady stay with us," Valerie said. "Sasha will be so happy to have the opportunity to play with Brady on a daily basis. I'll take them to Dog Beach whenever I can. Those two dogs just love to romp on the beach together. Charles and I enjoy being with them there too. We find going to Dog Beach is great way to get some fresh air and unwind. Just enjoy yourself with Jason in Napa valley and let us entertain Brady and Sasha," she said. "Thank you so much," Stephanie replied. "I know Brady will be delighted to be with you and Sasha. It will be a vacation for him too. I'll be glad to reciprocate whenever you and Charles take a vacation. The two dogs probably wish we would take vacations more often so they can be together."

Valerie would be glad to have Jason out of the office. She could then relax knowing he would not be there to compete with her for clients. She was amazed by the degree of stress relief she experienced just contemplating his absence from the firm. Indeed it confirmed the fact he was the major stressor in her life. She would celebrate his departure.

The trip from the San Jose airport to Napa in their rented convertible was easy and refreshing for Jason and Stephanie. Entering the grounds of the Silverado Resort and Spa they were both impressed by its elegance and beauty. Jason had arranged for a two day inclusive Silverado Escape

Package which included accommodation in a beautiful one bedroom fireplace suite, one round of golf and a 50 minute spa treatment per night's stay. Settling into their suite, Jason gave her a hug and a long passionate kiss. "Welcome to Napa Valley Stephanie," he murmured into her ear. "Jason I think I must be dreaming. This is so amazingly beautiful," she said. He had arranged for a fruit basket and a bottle of 1997 Silver Oak Cabernet Sauvignon to be ready in the suite. Pouring her a glass of wine he said, "It's really too early to drink this, but let's taste it anyway." She agreed and they toasted to each other as they savored the incredible bouquet and flavor of the wine.

After drinking one half bottle of the Silver Oak Cabernet Sauvignon, they decided to tour the grounds of the Silverado Resort and Spa. What they observed surprised and impressed them. There were two 18 hole championship PGA golf courses and 17 tennis courts. Looking at the tennis courts, Jason fleetingly remembered his humiliating defeat by the very capable tennis playing of Valerie Goldin. He quickly dispelled the thought. He didn't want to entertain any thoughts of Valerie during this vacation. Stephanie had noticed his fleeting frown and asked. "Is there something wrong?" "No, nothing at all," he replied. She knew he was hiding something. She surmised it had something to do with tennis. It was one of the only sports in which he didn't excel.

They counted 10 swimming pools! Entering the spa they were given a tour by an elegant Swedish lady who introduced herself as Heidi. "We have 16 treatment rooms, a well equipped exercise room and a 50 meter heated lap pool. This is our beauty salon and cafe," she said. "We will definitely be back later this afternoon to take advantage of all these amenities," Jason said. "We'll look forward to your return visit with us. We'll pamper you and I think you'll love it," Heidi cooed. As they left the spa facility, Stephanie turned to Jason and smiling said. "Yes, we will definitely return and soon!" "Absolutely," he replied. "I think you will enjoy a Swedish massage and a facial. But look over the palette of choices and chose whatever you desire. This is your birthday celebration and I want it to be luxurious and special." "Just being with you is special. The rest is all fluff, but I admit it's luxurious fluff," she said.

After touring the grill and restaurant, they returned to their room. "I think we should have lunch at the grill and then play nine holes of golf together. Does that sound inviting to you?" he asked. "That sounds great. Let me change into my golf outfit and I'll be ready to go," she said. After they ate a light lunch, they left for the golf course.

Jason had already arranged for a tee time. They drove their golf cart up to the first tee and gazed out over the beautiful, gently rolling fairway. Jason looked like a professional golfer as he drove his ball 275 yards straight down the fairway. "What an incredible drive," Stephanie said. "Valerie could never compete with you in golf only in tennis." Jason felt like he was stung by a wasp. It was though the stinger was still embedded in his flesh. Observing Jason's distress Stephanie asked. "Why did that remark upset you?" "Soon after we joined the Kaplan firm together Valerie challenged me to a tennis match. I didn't know she had been a tennis champion at Stanford." "What happened Jason?" "She destroyed me in front of a large crowd at the La Jolla Recreational Center. She was so quick around the court and her strokes were smooth and effortless. She's was only about five foot six and couldn't have weighed more than 125 pounds, yet she hit the ball harder than I did. Her timing and coordination were perfect. I was humiliated." "But that was over twenty years ago. Don't be ridiculous. Get over it." Stephanie said. Stephanie just didn't understand him. His loss to Valerie was still a festering wound. His life was based upon successful competition and not cooperation. He had to win and be the best. He hated to lose even if it was an insignificant tennis match. From that day on he had determined to dominate Valerie especially in the field of investments. He was proud of the way he was so successfully accomplishing that goal.

Jason drove their golf cart to the woman's tee. Stephanie drove her ball 175 yards straight down the fairway. "That's a very nice drive, Stephanie," Jason said. Her face beamed relishing his compliment.

It was a bright and sunny day. The air was fresh moved by a gentle warm breeze. Although his swing appeared effortless, Jason was putting 220 pounds of solid body rotation through the club into the golf ball which had to be frightened right before impact. "Playing golf is my equivalent of engaging in Tai Chi," he said. "You see to my way of thinking, the graceful rhythm of my golf swing matches Tai Chi movements."

Stephanie laughed "I suppose you have a mantra too." "I do," he replied. "What is it?" she asked. "Accelerate." "What kind of mantra is that?" Stephanie asked. "As my club face approaches the ball in its downward trajectory I whisper 'accelerate.' At impact the head of my golf club is reaching its maximum velocity and you just witnessed the result." In some ways Stephanie realized that the word accelerate characterized Jason's life. His successful option trades "accelerated" his income. He tried hard to speed up the acquisition of new clients. She wished he would hurry up and marry her! That was her most precious desire.

They joked and laughed together sharing stories and making plans as they covered the nine holes. Jason was only one over par for the round. Stephanie said she was not counting her strokes even though Jason was. He tallied a respectable 10 over par for her. He thought that was pretty impressive given the difficulty of the course.

They returned to their room, showered and changed into clothes suitable for the spa. Jason spent 20 minutes in the exercise room before having a steam bath followed by a Shiatsu massage. Stephanie had a 50 minute Swedish massage followed by a full treatment facial. The esthetician had designed the perfect combination based upon her skin type. It mainly consisted of cleansing, exfoliation, and hydration. They decided to forego swimming in the lap pool and retired to their suite. "This is an incredible resort and spa Jason. You selected the perfect place to celebrate my birthday," she said. "Which isn't until tomorrow," he said. She could only imagine what his fertile brain had devised, but she knew it would be special. "Let's have dinner and then come back to our room for appetizers," Jason said. Stephanie could only guess what the appetizers were. She hoped he was thinking that she was the appetizer he had in mind.

After a delicious dinner, they returned to their suite. Jason lit the fireplace and put on a CD containing some of Stephanie's favorite songs.

They were enjoying the rest of the Silver Oak 1997 Cabernet Sauvignon when Jason turned on the warm water to partially fill the bath tub. He added lavender bubble bath crystals and placed a padded towel over the back end of the tub. Next he lit scented candles throughout the bathroom and the bedroom. Helping her into the tub he had her lean back to rest her neck and head on the padded towel. Then he removed his clothes except for his shorts. Taking a soft sponge he gently caressed her body. "Jason, why don't you join me in the tub?" she asked. "I would love to, but I'm too big to fit into the tub with you already in there," he said. She looked up at his muscular body with admiration. Faint sensual sensations began to surge through her body. "You're probably right, but it would be fun trying," she remarked. "I wish the tub were larger. I would love to hold you and let the bubbles flow over our bodies," he replied. Stephanie was totally relaxed as he helped her out of the tub and wrapped a warm towel around her. "How did you get this towel warm?" Stephanie asked. "I placed it into the microwave oven for 65 seconds," he said. "You what?" she exclaimed. "I pulled out the towel from the microwave oven after 65 seconds had elapsed and it was warmed perfectly. Don't you agree?" he said. She mused. It was perfect. She was impressed by his ingenuity. She would have used the clothes dryer, but the towel was genuinely warm and luxurious.

The fireplace was glowing and an appealing fragrance filled the bedroom. A song with beautiful lyrics was playing which enhanced the atmosphere. He placed her face down on some towels spread out on the bed sheets. "Now it is my turn to give you a full body birthday massage," he murmured. She thought if this was the prelude to her birthday, she loved it. Removing the heated towel, he placed some warm scented massage oil on his hands and gently pressed them over her back, shoulders, and neck. She completely relaxed. He continued the massage moving down to her buttocks, thighs, lower legs and feet. His hands were strong yet gentle and soothing. "That feels so good," she murmured. "Now roll over on your back and I will continue your massage," he said. She willingly complied and he massaged the back then the front of her neck. He proceeded to gently massage her chest, then her breasts. She became warm all over. He continued down to her abdomen, pelvis, thighs and lower legs. She became sexually excited and urged him to join her in bed. He slipped off his shorts and they embraced followed by a passionate kiss. Perfectly entwined they made love, at first slowly and then with mounting intensity. Jason whispered, "I love you Stephanie." "I love you too Jason," she replied. It was the start of the most wonderful birthday present she had ever received. They fell asleep wrapped in each other's arms. It was a night they would always cherish.

# Chapter 21

WHEN THEY AWAKENED together the following morning, they reaffirmed their love for one another. "Happy birthday Stephanie," Jason exclaimed. "Thank you, Jason," she replied. Yes, today was her birthday and she could hardly wait to find out what activities Jason had planned for them to enjoy. Jason suggested she dress warmly in slacks, a blouse and a light sweater for they were going on a morning balloon ride over the Napa Valley.

They ascended in their hot air balloon and rose up to a height that gave them a grand view of the valley below. They looked down on myriads of vineyards each displaying an incredible palette of reds, greens, and golds. Passing over quaint towns their guide identified them as Yountville, Oakville, Rutherford, St. Helena and Calistoga. Valerie wanted to visit each of them. They were at peace with the world and with one another. The gentle breezes carried them across the majestic valley. As they wandered through space, their love for one another grew even deeper.

Once the balloon landed they enjoyed a delicious champagne brunch together. Their cares were being banished by the effects of the alcohol. Before the balloon trip started Jason had made sure that the bottle of Schramsberg Blanc de Blancs had arrived as it was to be exclusively served to them during the brunch following the trip. As she sipped the sparkling wine, Jason quipped. "Stephanie did you know that a bottle of Schramsberg Blanc de Blancs similar to this one helped normalize diplomatic relationships between the USA and The Peoples Republic of China?" "No, how in the world did that happen?" she asked. "In February 1972 President Nixon proposed 'A toast of Peace' with sparkling wine from a bottle of Schramsberg Blanc de Blancs. He was celebrating with the Chinese Premier Zhou Enlai in China. Later in the same week President Nixon and Henry Kissinger met with Mao Zedong, the Chairman of the Peoples Republic of China. You may recall that the Chinese Civil War had occurred 22 years earlier and Chiang Kai Shek had fled to Taiwan. Mainland China became a communist country. The USA had earlier recognized the Taiwanese government as the official Chinese regime. Nixon wanted to improve relationships with the mainland Peoples Republic of China to help buffer the communist power of the Soviet Union. Eventually that happened and slowly the Soviet Union crumbled. The Berlin Wall was eventually destroyed and there was a spinoff of several member states of the Soviet Bloc," he said. "I remember when the Berlin Wall was battered down," Stephanie replied. "Those pictures of people with sledge hammers and picks were circulated around the world. It was a glorious day for those living in both Western and Eastern Berlin." "I had the privilege of visiting Berlin soon after the Berlin Wall came down," Jason said. "There was a stark contrast between the two sides of the wall. Western Berlin was a thriving metropolis made up of industrious and wealthier people. Eastern Berlin contained bleak, gloomy buildings and mostly stolid, weary and poor people. The capitalist economic system was vibrant. The communist system based upon a centralized government was stagnant. What is now so interesting to me is how the current mainland Communist Chinese government has blended the two to create an economic powerhouse."

Stephanie encouraged Jason's glimpses into past history. "Why have you studied these developments?" she asked. "Companies and economies thrive by embracing new ideas and innovation," he replied. "I often invest in companies that create new products. Fortunes can be made using advanced option strategies in such companies. Often new startup companies are based upon a great idea or product, but they don't have enough capital to finance their operations. Angel investors step in to provide the needed seed capital and the angel investors are granted shares and warrants in return. If the company is successful, it may eventually offer an IPO or Initial Public Offering. Sometimes the start up is acquired by a larger, well established company at a premium share price. The original partners and angel investors can achieve an incredible return from their original shares and warrants. It's through situations like these that overnight millionaires are created," he said. "If the company fails, the investment becomes worthless. I look hard for these investment opportunities. It's one of the reasons I joined a San Diego based angel investing group." "Have any of your investments through the angel group paid off?" Stephanie asked. "Yes and some have failed. The exit strategies are often prolonged and the original investment dollars remain stagnant if that occurs. That's one reason I primarily invest in rather short term options as a way to keep my personal investment dollars and those of my clients active. In both circumstances timing is crucial. But let's forget all that and enjoy our next adventure," he said.

Jason wanted stark contrasts to occur during this trip. The sedentary balloon ride was replaced by a thrilling jet ski ride on Lake Berryessa located to the northeast of Napa. Jason had driven for an hour and pulled up at the Capella Cove boat ramp at Lake Berryessa. There he was met by Michael May who owned a modern jet ski designed to hold two people. Jason had rented it for the next two hours. Stephanie assessed the situation and declared. "Jason I'm not dressed for this!" "I know that as he closed up the top of their rental convertible. Just hop in the back seat and change into the new bathing suit you'll find there," he said. "What? You bought me a new bathing suit," she said. "Yes I have and you'll look terrific in it," he exclaimed. And he was right. When she stepped out of the car both Jason and Michael whistled their approval. It was a brightly colored floral pattern and it fit her perfectly. With her flowing blond hair, bright blue eyes, and attractive face, she still turned eyes at 44.

After fastening their life preservers, Jason and Stephanie took off down the lake. Jason let out a whoop and Stephanie wrapped her arms around him holding him tightly. They explored the coves along the 26 miles of the lake, sometimes stopping to moor the jet ski and walk into the woods just for a change of scenery. The natural beauty of the surroundings was magical. They were carefree and in love. It was quite a change from the stream of cars working their way up the Napa Valley and they loved it. Stephanie realized that Jason somehow knew how to please her with his adventuresome spirit and innovative ideas. He was a unique man and she felt lucky to have him.

Returning to the Silverado Resort and Spa they still had time to play another nine holes golf. This time it was challenging for Jason and a nightmare for Stephanie. She landed in a sand trap on five of the nine holes and had a horrible time escaping from them. Jason as usual was both long and accurate. On this occasion he was one under par. Even the golf pro was impressed when he saw Jason's score card. "You could potentially become a professional golfer," he said. "I only play golf to relax," Jason said. "Well I don't think your fellow golfers would want to bet against you," the pro responded. "I give them plenty of strokes and we usually come out pretty even," Jason said. That wasn't entirely true. He usually did win. For him winning was important.

Stephanie was proud of him. He was so strong and masculine. She looked forward to sharing the bed again with him later that evening. First they had another session in the spa. Jason enjoyed the steam bath and afterwards swam a few laps in the heated lap pool. He was completely refreshed and excited over the evening he had planned for Stephanie.

Jason had reserved dinner for them on the Napa Valley Wine Train. They boarded the train at 6:15 pm and departed the station at exactly 6:30. It was still light out and they enjoyed the scenery from their booth in the Vista Dome. As they passed famous wineries, they both realized the importance of vacations. It was a time to unwind and to enjoy one another. They also realized that they were very hungry not having eaten any lunch. Looking over the menu Stephanie selected the grilled shrimp as her Hors d'oeuvre. Her first course was a beet Carpaccio salad. For her main course she picked the seared Muscovy duck breast. Finally for desert she selected the cream Brule with fresh berries. Jason skipped the shrimp but selected the same salad Stephanie had ordered. For his main course he chose the roasted beef tenderloin wrapped in bacon with shallots. His desert was a tiramisu truffle enrobed in a dome of chocolate. With each of the individual servings Jason had the sommelier provide them with a suitable wine.

Jason excused himself for a few minutes and then reappeared with the executive chef. After he was introduced to Stephanie, the chef produced a beautiful birthday cake and asked the surrounding guests to join him in singing happy birthday to her. They readily obliged and Stephanie was brought to tears of happiness. "Jason, you think of everything," she said. "I try." Then he pulled out a specially wrapped gift box for her to open. Nervously she pulled it open and pulled out a gorgeous pendant containing a beautiful sapphire surrounded by diamonds. She gasped. "Jason, it's so beautiful." He helped to clasp it around her neck. Two women sitting in a booth across from them rose and walked over to congratulate her. Perhaps it was just an excuse to get a closer look at her handsome companion rather than the incredible pendant, she mused, but she thanked them anyway. What woman wouldn't want to spend time with Jason, she thought.

"The next time we take this train I'll arrange to have it occur on the Mystery Night," Jason said. "Clues to solve the mystery are presented to the guests during the course of the scenes. Solving the mystery is a challenge. Would you enjoy that?" he asked. "That would be fun. Does it take place very often?" she asked. "No it occurs only about once a month, but I could reserve a spot for us in advance," he replied. Just like he had done tonight, she thought. He was a great planner. She wondered what else he had in store for her in the Napa Valley.

They dis-embarked the train at 9:30 PM and drove back to their suite. They could hardly wait to indulge in the excitement and passion of the previous night, but it happened again. The ecstasy they experienced that night left them deeply in love and completely satisfied as they drifted off to sleep.

# Chapter 22

AFTER CHECKING OUT of the Silverado Resort and Spa the next day, Jason and Stephanie first drove to the Jessel Gallery in Napa. Jason was immediately struck by the rich colors of the goddesses portrayed in the works by Jessel Miller. Unfortunately all of her original watercolors had been acquired. He would not be satisfied with a print or giclee. The same was true for her landscapes. The originals had all been purchased. He considered making a private appointment with either Jessel Miller or Timothy David Dixon to commission a Napa Valley landscape. He admired the way they both blended beautiful colors into their landscapes. "Look at the wonderful illustrations in Jessel Miller's books," Stephanie said. "They are beautiful," Jason replied. Stephanie decided to buy the entire Jessel book collection for her library. "What an exceptional art gallery," Stephanie said. After exploring the rest of the multifaceted gallery, they finally decide to leave and continue their trip.

Driving north on the Silverado trail there first stop was the Crouching Lion Winery. Entered the driveway to the winery, Stephanie exclaimed. "Look at the statue of the crouching lion Jason. It's full of energy and vitality." "It's rather stunning," he said. "It certainly is. I hope the wines are as impressive as the lion," she said. Jason cautioned Stephanie to only taste the wine and dump the rest in the spittoon. They entered the tasting room and Jason said. "I try to savor the aroma of the wine by first swirling it for 30 seconds. Then I place my nose into the wine glass resting it on my forehead. Sniffing the bouquet I enjoy all of the aromas. This is especially important with the full bodied Cabernet Sauvignon wines. Then I place a small portion of the wine on my tongue and swish it around for 10 to 15 seconds savoring the flavors. Passing some air over the wine by gently inhaling I let the wine drift further back on my palate trying to identify its complex flavors before I swallow it. It takes some practice, but this technique has enhanced my enjoyment of wine," he said. Stephanie tried it and almost choked. "It's the inhaling of air over my tongue that chokes me," she said. "I can't seem to get it right." "As I say, it does take practice. You'll get the hang of it before the week is over I'm sure," he said. "Remember we are only tasting and not drinking the wine." Guests were gathering around the bar telling stories. They decided to join in and thoroughly enjoyed themselves. This was living at its best, Stephanie thought. They tasted the best Cabernets and Merlots offered by the establishment of the Crouching Lion before deciding to leave and to continue their trip northbound.

Reaching the road they let several bicyclists and cars pass before turning left into the northbound lane of the Silverado Trail. It was a bright, sunny day and they were happy. After driving a few miles, they saw a car suddenly burst out of a driveway just a block ahead of them. It turned right to go north in their same lane. The white sedan swerved menacingly half way into the southbound lane before regaining control. Over compensating the driver drove into the bike lane and gunned the engine. The car weaved as it sped forward. Then there was a terrible crash and Jason and Stephanie both screamed as they watched the car smash into a bicyclist catapulting the rider off to the right. "The driver isn't stopping Jason. He's racing ahead to get away!" "Can you get the license number?" Jason asked. "No, it's impossible. He's too far away for me to see it," she said. Pulling off to the side of the road behind the scene of the accident, Jason and Stephanie dashed forward to help the injured victim. They were aghast when they saw the grotesque shape of a pretty lady her face splattered in blood. A young man was cradling her in his arms and sobbing. "No, No!" he cried. "Couldn't he see we were in the bike lane? It's broad daylight," he wailed. Jason quickly assessed the hideously injured lady and called 911. "Get an ambulance and the police to northbound Silverado Trail about 4 miles north of the Crouching Lion winery. There's been a terrible accident. A car has smashed into a woman bicyclist and has left the scene without stopping," he said. Jason turned to the woman and checked her carotid artery pulse. He was shocked as it was absent. Turning to Stephanie he whispered. "I'm afraid she's dead. She's been killed, actually murdered by a drunken driver. I'd like to get my hands on him," he exclaimed angrily. The driver had narrowly missed the husband, Brady Nelson, who had been bicycling five yards in front of his wife but farther to the right in the bike lane. That position had saved his life.

Stephanie wanted to console Brady, but she was at a loss for words. "Melanie, Melanie," he cried. Stephanie could not bear to look at Melanie's mangled body and turned away crying. "That crazy, drunken maniac," she screamed. "He wouldn't even stop to help. That's terrible." She picked up some gravel and hurled it away. A few cars had now stopped and more people began to gather around the scene horrified by what they saw.

Within 10 minutes the siren of the ambulance pierced the valley floor and pulled up alongside them. The medics jumped out of the vehicle and raced to the victim's side. After they examined her, they confirmed that she was dead. Brady shrieked. "It's not only Melanie who is dead. It's also our unborn son." "Oh my God," Stephanie screamed. "Your son?" "Yes, our son. Melanie was 3 months pregnant today. It was going to be our first child," he cried. "Please get the savage who killed them. Please find him," he said as he buried his head into Melanie's bosom. Both Jason and Stephanie were furious. Their disgust toward the driver increased with time. Although it was hard, Jason took pictures of the twisted bike and mangled body of Melanie Brady. He wanted to record the devastation the hit and run driver had caused.

Jason glanced at his watch. It was 12:45 PM in the early afternoon when the police arrived just moments after the ambulance. The medics informed Officer O'Reilly that the female bicyclist was dead. "Are there any witnesses to the accident?" he asked. Both Jason and Stephanie stepped forward and stated that they had witnessed a white sedan barrel out of the driveway about 1/4 mile to the south of them. They described how the car was weaving when it struck the victim on her bicycle. "She was clearly in the bike lane when he hit her," they said. "And he didn't even pause," Stephanie exclaimed. "In fact he gunned the car to get away." Officer O'Reilly put out an all out alert. "Be on the lookout for a white sedan with damage to its right front end last seen driving north on the Silverado Trail about 20 minutes ago. It's a hit and run and the woman bicycle victim is dead. We don't have a license number and the actual driver was not visualized," he said. "I think it was a man," Brady said. "I just saw a glimpse of him as he shot by me. I can't give you any details. It was just a fleeting glance and then I rushed to my wife. I thought he would at least stop. Instead he increased his speed and fled. I tried to get the license plate, but he was too far away."

Jason exchanged business cards with Officer O'Reilly and also gave one to Brady. "Call me on my cell phone if I can be of more help," he said. "I will be glad to testify against him if you catch him. By the way it just occurred to me. He obviously had been drinking at the winery whose road he emerged from just down the road. The bar tender may be able to provide you with credit card slips from some of his last customers as well as descriptions. His bill must have been settled within the last 30 to 40 minutes." "That's exactly what I've been thinking," Officer O'Reilly said. "And that's exactly what I'm going to do next, Mr. Gianelli. Thank you for bringing it up." Then officer O'Reilly startled them. "By the way have the two of you been drinking?" he asked. "Yes, we recently tasted wine at the Crouching Lion," Jason remarked. "If you only tasted the wine, you won't mind if I test you with the Breath Analyzer," he replied. "We won't mind at all," Jason said. They both passed and Officer O'Reilly smiled. "I only did this because if we capture the suspect, he may claim that the witnesses were drunk. This proves that you were both sober," he said. Jason and Stephanie were both relieved and thanked Officer O' Reilly for thinking of that angle. "May I call you later this afternoon to check on your progress?" Jason asked Officer O'Reilly. "Yes, of course," he said. "We may have to change our plans if you need us for any reason," Jason said. "I understand and I appreciate your cooperation," the officer said.

As they left the scene of the accident, Jason took a last look at the grieving husband, Brady Nelson. Jason was fuming and Stephanie was quietly crying. "Jason, she was so young and pretty. And besides she was pregnant with their first child. What a tragedy." Jason was thinking of Judy, his ex wife who had refused to bear him children. He had yearned for a son and a daughter. He could only imagine what kind of reaction he would have had if Judy had been killed while pregnant. Rage consumed his thinking. "There must be some way we can track down this killer," he said. "I'm not a detective, Jason. I don't know what the police will do, but they will probably devise ways of tracking him down. Your idea about checking the wine receipts was brilliant," she said. "Reviewing them should provide some leads. Don't you agree?" Jason was deliberating over the issue. "Yes, I think if they can assemble some names, they might be able to come up with the most likely suspect. Let's see if the police can nab him within the next day or two," he said.

# Chapter 23

ALTHOUGH THEY WERE somber, Jason could not pass by the Stag's Leap Wine Cellars entrance. The winery consistently produced some of his favorite wines. As a wine connoisseur, Jason remarked. "Stephanie, I want to tell you a famous story about Stag's Leap Wine Cellars. A wine event of great historical importance occurred in 1976 in Paris. A famous blind wine tasting was held comparing the best French Bordeaux Cabernet Sauvignons and Chardonnays with those from California. Nine French wine tasters with impeccable professional standards were chosen to sample the wines blindly with their wine labels covered up and rank them from first to last place. The French were stunned by the results. The 1973 Stag's Leap Wine Cellars Cabernet Sauvignon was ranked first. Four of the top ranked Bordeaux Cabernets were defeated. Besides that the 1973 Chateau Montelana Chardonnay from Napa Valley had bested its French counterparts. The California wines were catapulted unto the world stage and have remained there ever since." "But did their Cabernet age well?" Stephanie asked. "Yes it aged beautifully. In fact it only moved down one notch to second place 30 years later when the Paris competition was reenacted. The exact wines and vintages from the original competition were again tasted blindly. The 18 expert wine tasting panelists were internationally celebrated names in wine," he said. "What were the results?" Stephanie asked. "Incredibly the top five wines came from California. It confirmed the fact that California based wines aged extremely well." "How exciting!" Stephanie exclaimed. "Yes, it was electrifying," Jason said. "Even in the blind tasting of contemporary wines judged on the same day, the Stag's Leap Wine Cellars Cask 23 Cabernet Sauvignon placed first in the UK panel and second among California's leading Cabernet Sauvignon producers in the combined panel." "No wonder you wanted to stop here for some wine tasting," Stephanie remarked.

Someday Jason thought he would make enough money to purchase his own Napa Valley winery. It was an ambitious thought but not beyond his reach. That desire would serve to drive his ongoing quest for more successful option trades.

After spending some time shopping in Yountville, they checked into the Bardessono Resort and Spa. Later they ate a delicious meal in Lucy's restaurant located right in the hotel. Back in their suite, Jason picked up his cell phone and called Officer O'Reilly who immediately answered. "Have you picked up any leads from the winery receipts?" Jason asked. "Yes we have," O'Reilly said. "The management at the Clarion Napa Valley Winery has been very cooperative. Only three groups of people had settled their bills during the time frame we defined. They consisted of a sedate older couple, four British business men, and a loud, boisterous man who they had cut off serving because he was drunk. We think the drunk is our suspect. We have his name and we are in the process of surveying our data base to find out more about him. Now it's a matter of locating him and the car he was driving." "That's great news!" Jason said. "Well we haven't caught him, but we will," O'Reilly said. "May I keep in touch with you?" Jason asked. "Of course you can. You are our chief witnesses and we don't want to lose you."

"Stephanie, the police have identified the most likely hit and run suspect! They are trying to track him down," he said. "How do you think they'll do that?" she asked. "If it were me, I would first survey all of the surrounding car rental agencies for a white sedan rental taken out over the past week. Then I would check all of the auto repair shops in town and around this area. He will most likely have the damage to the right front of his rental car completely repaired to cover up the evidence and also to avoid suspicion from the rental agency. I think he will avoid auto repair shops in Napa. He probably will go to Santa Rosa or even as far as Sacramento to have the car damage repaired," he said. "You're probably right," Stephanie said. "He won't want to stay around here and take the chance of being identified. I hope no one else was injured during his intoxicated state." "Maybe he stopped at a bed and breakfast to sober up before leaving the area," Jason said. "He wouldn't want to be captured drunk because his fines and sentencing would be significantly worse."

# Chapter 24

THE NEXT MORNING at breakfast Jason called Officer O'Reilly again. "Have you made any progress in the Melanie Nelson case?" he asked. "Yes we have. We have traced his car rental to Didactic Car Rental located at the at the San Francisco Airport terminal. He's scheduled to return it in three days. We'll be waiting for him if we don't apprehend him sooner," he said. "What's his name?" Jason asked. "I won't give that to you," Officer O'Reilly said. "I will say that he turns out to be a prominent defense attorney who lives in Beverly Hills, California. That will potentially make it more difficult to prosecute him. He'll hire the best defense attorney he can find and he probably knows them all." "But he'll be convicted. Won't he?" Jason asked. "Yes he will. He'll be charged with a felony hit and run offense. If you want to see the potential penalties, I suggest you go online and click felony hit and run. I think we'll get a conviction and he won't like the consequences," he said. "Thanks for the follow up," Jason replied. "May I call you again tomorrow in further follow up?" "Yes of course you can. We'll need your testimonies to convict this lawyer. He'll rue the day he killed Melanie Nelson and their son."

Jason relayed what he had learned to Stephanie. They finished eating and returned to their suite. Jason connected his computer to the internet. He smiled as he reviewed the potential felony hit and run consequences. "Stephanie when they catch this defense attorney he will face a fine of up to $10,000 dollars. I don't think will that will faze him, but he killed Melanie Nelson and their child. That will result in his imprisonment in a California

State prison for up to four years, perhaps even longer. Then there is also a monetary restitution settlement to Brady Nelson for the loss of his wife and unborn son. That will be determined in a civil not a criminal court. The jury and judge could declare a large sum of money is due to Brady Nelson. But how do you place a monetary figure on the death and loss of a wife and son? What are they worth?" Jason asked. "To Brady, everything," Stephanie replied.

Jason was surprised to learn that felony cases may involve eight separate court appearances and numerous filings. After the initial arraignment on the complaint which occurs within 72 hours of arrest, the defendant is read the formal charges issued against him. It could take many weeks before a jury trial takes place and then more time before the judge determines sentencing. "We won't know when or where we will testify in this case Stephanie," Jason said. "But in the meantime let's try to explore more of Napa Valley and enjoy ourselves. I want to pursue activities that add laughter and joy to our lives." Stephanie agreed. She had just witnessed Melanie's untimely death. She wanted to enjoy her time with Jason. She realized that no one ever knows exactly when their life may end.

Jason outlined a rather extensive winery tour to Stephanie with the warning that they would only enjoy the aromas and a small tasting of each wine serving to avoid any signs of inebriation. Stephanie whole heartily agreed and they set off. Jason had secured advanced reservations for two Robert Mondavi winery tours. During the first tour Jason wanted Stephanie to learn how to read wine labels, the reasons for swirling the wine in the glass, and how to smell, taste and describe wine. After the course ended, Stephanie remarked. "Jason this course has been extraordinary. I have a much better understanding and appreciation of the subtleties involved in enjoying wine now. The wine educator made everything so clear." "These speakers are experts in their field," Jason said. "That's why I wanted you to come here in order to get better educated."

"I have another tour reserved for us. It's called the Signature Tour and Tasting. In this tour we will follow the path of the grape from its start in the vineyard to the cellar and then to the finished wine. It will give you insights into the entire wine making process," he said. The initial part of the Signature Tour took them to the To Kalon vineyard. "This is celebrated as one of the finest first-growth vineyards in the world." "Robert Mondavi must have been an exceptional man to create this winery," Stephanie remarked. "He was," Jason said. "He was a truly remarkable man who left an incredible legacy. He was 94 years old when he died in 2008."

Entering the winemaking cellars the tour guide gave an in depth explanation of the fermentation and barrel aging aspects of wine making. Toward the end of the tour they sat down and were treated to three wines. The educational specialist described and demonstrated the techniques he recommended for deriving the most pleasure from the aromas, flavors and textures of the wine they were sampling. "I have been enjoying some of the finest wines in the world over the past 10 years," Jason said. "When we return to La Jolla it will be my pleasure to share with you wines from my private collection. That will include a bottle of the 1997 Robert Mondavi Cabernet Sauvignon Reserve, one of my favorites. Now that you are learning how to maximize the wine drinking experience you will appreciate some of my classic vintages even more."

"The next time we come back to this winery I will arrange for their Twilight Tour. At the end of that tour there is a tasting of their reserve and featured wines accompanied by an exceptional cheese board." "That sounds wonderful," Stephanie said. "Should I begin making arrangements for a return birthday trip one year from now?" Jason asked. "Yes, please arrange it. I would love to have another trip to Napa Valley with you," she replied.

"Well there are more surprises in store for you over the next two days," he replied. "They will have to be spectacular to match what I have already experienced," she said.

"One of the largest fund raisers in the country occurs each year in this valley. It's called the Napa Valley Wine Auction and it raises millions of dollars annually for charities. I attended the spectacular event in 2008, and I bought several thousand dollars worth of wine at that auction. The money went to worthy causes and I also secured some excellent bottles of wine. I met a delightful couple, Tom and Martha May, at the auction and we became friends. They treated me to a fabulous dinner at their local country club and introduced me to a bottle of Vintage 1986 Martha's Vineyard Heitz Cellar's Cabernet Sauvignon." "Is there any connection between Martha and Tom May and that bottle of wine?" Stephanie asked. "Yes, the grapes actually came from their own vineyard and the wine was exceptional! They were very generous in sharing their wine with me and taking me to dinner. I enjoyed spending time with them and I hope we'll be able to visit them on this trip as they have remained close friends."

"Stephanie, if you want to learn more about the life of Robert Mondavi, I suggest you read his autobiography. It's beautifully written. I have a copy in my library at home and you are welcome to borrow it," Jason said. "I would love to do that," she replied. "The charities supported by Robert Mondavi and his wife, Margrit, will certainly preserve their legacy," Jason said.

# Chapter 25

THE FOLLOWING DAY they drove to the Grgich Hills Estate, a celebrated Rutherford winery. Their estate grown wines were deliciously created from grapes grown in their certified organic and bio-dynamic vineyards. "It would be such an honor to meet Miljenko 'Mike' Grgich, the patriarch of Grigch Hills, Stephanie," Jason said. "He was the noted winemaker that helped produce the Chateau Montelena 1973 Chardonnay. Remember I mentioned earlier it was the vintage that won first place among the white burgundies and chardonnays entered into the 'Judgement of Paris' blind wine tasting competition in 1976. I believe he turned 87 years old earlier this year in April 2010."

After enjoying two excellent wine tastings at Grgich Hills, Jason suggested something different. "Let's go stomp on some grapes Stephanie!" he said. They kicked off their shoes and indeed did tromp on Grgich Cabernet Sauvignon grapes. They burst out laughing as they danced together over the grapes. It was a hilarious sight and they loved the action. They heard a beautiful melody playing in the background. Catching the cadence of the song they began to coordinate their dynamic stomping movements into a rhythmic response. Stephanie's face exploded with joy and laughter. She embraced the immediate moments of pleasure. The barrel of grapes became a vehicle for her joy. She was totally released from worldly worries and cares as she felt the pure pleasure of dancing over the grapes.

Even the more critical and logical Jason Gianelli relaxed and let himself go. Crushing grapes with his feet in this beautiful setting with the woman he loved lifted his spirits. His life was dominated by his quest to gain prosperity, prestige and power. It was his current success in realizing these goals that allowed him to enjoy these moments of freedom.

As they stepped out of the wine barrel, they placed their stained purple feet on souvenir T shirts. Valerie giggled looking at their footprints on the T shirts. Jason was amused too and a broad grin lit up his face. "Jason I dare you to wear this T shirt into your office when you return to La Jolla. Wouldn't your co-workers be surprised? I'll bet you would even get a laugh out of Valerie." Jason imagined the reactions of his cohorts. Most of them would just stare in disbelief. It would be so far out of character for Jason to dress that way. Yet he thought it would lend an element of surprise during one of his option seminars. He visualized himself suddenly tearing off his clean white shirt to display the funny purple footed T shirt lying underneath it. It would generate some laughter. Then he could explain that his successful option trades paid for his entire Napa Valley trip to the wineries. Next he would give a bottle of Grgich wine to each participant. What a great marketing plan. Perhaps he should incorporate it into his option seminar.

He turned to face Stephanie and said. "Your challenge has some potential. I'll think about it and maybe even do it." Creating laughter into a dry option lecture had its merits, he thought. It would loosen up the participants and make him more likeable.

"That was fun," Stephanie said. "Maybe we could get a job as grape stompers during the crush. It would be a nice reprieve from your option trading." "Yes, I could trade options in the morning and stomp grapes in the afternoon to relieve my tension," Jason said. A beautiful smile crossed his face and he chuckled. Stephanie looked at him more closely. She loved it when he loosened up and enjoyed himself. Back home he was so serious most of the time. She thought that this trip was good for him and for her too. They were having lots of fun together. She smiled thinking it would be wonderful if she could help him have fun and laugh everyday as his lifelong wife. But how could she get him to propose marriage?

Jason had made reservations at the Round Pond Estate winery for their Il Pranzo lunch. There they savored the local artisan cheeses, meats and breads. The fresh fruits and vegetables were delicious and came directly from the MacDonnell family owned orchard and garden. Besides their excellent wines the winery was unique having its own olive mill. They tasted their handcrafted olive oils and red wine vinegars. "I love dipping this gourmet bread into the different olive oils and vinegars," Stephanie said. "There are so many incredible flavors." "The wine goes well with them too," Jason said. They were enjoying some unique sensory experiences at Round Pond. It was a lunch that left them satisfied and satiated.

Before leaving Jason phoned Officer O'Reilly from the Round Pond terrace and asked for an update. "We have had a major breakthrough Mr. Gianelli," O'Reilly said. "Armed with the license plate number on the white sedan obtained from Didactic Car Rental agency, we were able to trace the rental car to a collision auto repair shop in Santa Rosa, California. We sent an undercover agent to the site. He informed me that they always take pictures of the damaged cars before and after they repair them. The car is scheduled to be picked up tomorrow. That's when we will be waiting in unmarked cars to apprehend and arrest him," he said. "That's incredible," Jason said. "What a saga. You and your team are to be commended for your excellent work." "We do our best," Officer O'Reilly said. "But it's not over yet. I think we are closing in on him. Assuming we are able to arrest him tomorrow, the trial date will be several weeks into the future. He will probably try to change the venue to Los Angeles which would probably be more convenient for his defense lawyer. But we will fight him on that too. This is where the accident occurred." "Whenever and wherever you need us to testify as witnesses against him we promise to fulfill our obligation," Jason said. "We want this savage to be incarcerated for a long time. We hope the fine and restitution settlement impoverish him. He deserves a harsh punishment for what he's done. Please call me tomorrow after you have him in custody." "I'll do that Mr. Gianelli and thank you for your interest and cooperation."

Jason turned to Stephanie and announced the great news. "The police should be able to arrest the hit and run driver tomorrow," he said. "They've traced the damaged white sedan to a collision body shop in Santa Rosa." "That's wonderful," she replied. "Wouldn't you like to be there when they arrest him?" she asked. "Yes, I would. He won't be happy," Jason said. "But even though he's desperate I doubt that he'll resist his arrest. That would only compound his problems which are already serious. I think we should celebrate by drinking some sparkling wine." With that in mind he took her to a winery made famous for producing exceptional sparkling wines.

Once they settled into their chairs they both lifted their flutes containing the bubbly and toasted. "I propose a toast to the successful capture of Melanie's killer tomorrow," Jason said. "I'll drink to that," Stephanie said. They both smiled broadly as they celebrated the thought of his capture.

Moving down the corridor of a gallery at the winery Jason was emotionally moved by the beautiful collection of photographs. "Stephanie, please study this photograph showing water cascading over a cliff. The photographer must have waited until the sun was shining brightly at a perfect angle to the cascading water and then took the picture. See how the water is illuminated," he said. "The light is captured perfectly to enhance the vitality of the currents flowing over the cliff. Also just look at all the variations of black and white shades in the photograph. The details are so precise and clear. It's truly incredible." "I agree," Stephanie said. She didn't appreciate the fine points of the photograph he had just shared with her. He discerned subtleties in art forms and wine that escaped her. She just enjoyed the emotional impact of a photograph, a painting or a fine tasting wine. She didn't have to compete with Jason. She would let Valerie engage in that hazardous endeavor.

Jason's enthusiasm made her glow because she saw him so happy. Stephanie realized that Jason was a much more complex and complicated man than she had originally thought. His mind was active and his tastes discerning. He was a student of history, art, photography, literature and of course option trading. As a wine connoisseur, he appreciated and enjoyed the finest wines. She felt privileged to have him in her life.

What Stephanie didn't know was Jason's dark side. He had gloated when the Friedmans had switched $3 million dollars from Valerie to him to manage. He never told Stephanie how he had hacked into Valerie's computer. He was proud of his nefarious and unethical behavior. Yes, he was adroit in hacking into computers, making profitable option trades, mocking his co-workers and hiding his actions from Stephanie. Domination of Valerie was one of his chief goals. He thought he was in love with

Stephanie, but was it real? Everything was suspect when it came to evaluating Jason.

How could Stephanie who was experiencing so much of Jason's love surmise that he also had such a black heart. She was mostly oblivious to the fact that he could be callous and devious. She had experienced a glimpse of that side of his character at the party he had held for his clients, their friends and Dr. and Mrs. Friedman. There she witnessed how he had downgraded Valerie in an attempt to gain more clients and especially the Friedman's account. She was now experiencing his charm and charismatic personality. Although Valerie had hinted that Jason could be deceitful and dishonest, Stephanie chose to ignore those postulated shortcomings. He was wonderful to her and that's what mattered.

Upon leaving this winery they drove to the beautiful Chappellet Winery located on Pritchard Hill. Jason had reserved a 3 pm tasting. They arrived late but were cordially greeted and invited into the tasting room. After tasting and savoring the exceptional Chappellet wines, Jason led Stephanie outdoors. "Just look at the incredible view of Lake Hennessey from this hilltop, Stephanie." "It's a wonderful sight, but so is this winery's magnificent garden. Just look at it," she said. The garden consisted of a potpourri of unusual shrubs, brightly colored flowers, and an interesting variety of plants that extended into the wilds of Pritchard Hill. A gentle warm breeze brushed across her face as she listened to the rustling leaves of beautiful large leaf maples, California live oaks, and Manzanita. A wild assortment of chirping birds were flitting about in the exquisite Madrone trees that graced the hillside. She enjoyed the wonders of nature.

Stephanie's thoughts turned to Brady, her Bichon Frise left behind with Valerie during her trip to Napa Valley. "Jason, I think Brady would love running around this hillside." "I'm sure he would. There are alot of exciting places to explore," he said. Brady was probably playing with Sasha, Valerie's frisky Yorkshire terrier on Dog Beach in Del Mar. She could visualize both Brady and Sasha with her here scampering up and down Pritchard hill together. What fun they would have dodging one another under the maple trees and live oaks. They had carefree lives nurtured by the love of their owners, Stephanie and Valerie. If only Valerie and Jason could enjoy one another in the same way she thought. Instead they were embroiled in an intense rivalry competing for investment clients. It was the unpleasant nature of their rivalry that was so disturbing to her. Valerie was her best friend and she loved Jason with all of her heart. What a dilemma. She felt helpless in trying to resolve their differences. She was failing as a peacemaker and that frustrated her. It was ironic she thought that Brady and Sasha so fully enjoyed one another while mature adults like Valerie and Jason were locked in a contentious battle.

Despite those thoughts she was at peace with herself. She realized that there was much more than just wine in the Napa Valley. There were incredibly beautiful gardens, landscapes, and a fabulous lake where she could enjoy jet skiing with Jason. Yes, she could savor the Napa Valley wines. She could also acknowledge the beauty of the vistas observed from their soaring balloon ride and from the hillsides. In fact the views from Pritchard hill were exceptional and she revered them. There was still more to it than that. In Napa Valley she was imbued with a reverence for life that surpassed her own understanding. What more could she want? "I'd like to come back here next year for my birthday, Jason." "I'll make sure that happens," he said.

Jason had secured a dinner reservation at the celebrated Auberge du Soleil known for its excellent cuisine prepared and directed by their prized executive chef. They were both hungry following the long day of wine hopping. "I'm going to have the Maine lobster for my first course followed by the Alaskan halibut," Stephanie said. She could hardly wait for the food to arrive. Jason also ordered the Maine lobster but chose the prime New York beef for his second course. "Let's share the wild flowered honey roasted figs for desert," Jason said. "What a fabulous meal. You know how to pick incredible restaurants," she said. "I thought you would especially like this one." "Each restaurant you have selected has been unique and wonderful. Thank you for sharing them with me." Stephanie reached over and touched his hand. It was a gentle touch from a beautiful soul and he felt it in his heart.

The vista from the Auberge du Soleil dining room situated in an open air patio overlooking the valley and surrounding hills was spectacular. They were entranced by the orange and golden hues emblazoned by the sun as it set in the west.

After the meal ended, a guide took them on a tour through one of the largest suites, the Champagne Private Maison. "Jason it's beautiful but I wouldn't want to leave it to visit the wineries," she said. This particular Maison was a luxurious 1800 square foot accommodation which included indoor and outdoor space. French doors led out to a trellised terrace equipped with a sunken hot tub. The master bedroom was spacious with a fireplace and sitting area. A sweeping view of the Napa Valley was offered from the king sized bed. The master bathroom even came with a steam shower for two and an oversized tub. "Look at the size of that tub Jason. It's perfect for the two of us," she said. Her mind had returned to their passionate first night at the Silverado Resort and Spa. Could they repeat that night here? She relished the thought. "I could live out the rest of my life right here," she exclaimed. Jason smiled. "Well we could try it for a night or two next year," he said. "I would love to stay here, but I foresee a problem. With the delicious food, hot tub, steam shower and other amenities, I would gain 25 pounds quickly and you wouldn't want to be seen with me," she said. "Don't worry about that," he replied. "My next door neighbor, Mrs. Brown got rid of one hundred and eighty six pounds of ugly, disgusting fat." "How in the world did she do that," Stephanie asked. "She divorced her husband." Stephanie smiled and laughed as Jason continued his banter. "Of course we could enjoy exercising together to lose the weight," Jason said. She noticed the mischievous grin that appeared on his face. She imagined what he meant and she blushed. Yes, she would look forward to returning to Auberge du Soleil next year.

Finally they decided to drive back to the Bardessono Hotel and Spa. They had considered going north to Calistoga for music and dancing. They loved to dance together. It was so very tempting. It was just so easy to take the Rutherford road cut off and drive south into Yountville. It had been a long day. With some reluctance they decided to forgo the music and dancing. Perhaps they could do it on another night or next year.

# Chapter 26

THE FOLLOWING MORNING during breakfast Jason's thoughts turned to Brady Nelson. He could only imagine the profound degree of grief and despair he must be experiencing. "You look sad Jason," Stephanie said. "Is there something wrong?" she asked. "I was just reflecting on the tragic death of Melanie Brady and her unborn son. I would share in Brady's loss if you were to die," he said. "Well I'm very much alive and intend to stay that way as long as I can. I have an appreciation of death too. When my husband died of metastatic colon cancer five years ago, I became deeply depressed and lonely. I went through some tough times," she said. "Today Melanie's killer may be finally captured and face incarceration. He needs to pay for his offensive and cowardly act. Speeding away from his accident scene instead of stopping to help is reprehensible. I hope they imprison him for a long time if they catch him," she said.

Contemplating that thought they signed out of the Bardessono Resort and Spa and drove north to register into the Harvest Inn for the next two nights. Jason had booked a room called the Spa Vineyard View with its king sized bed, large brick fireplace, private patio, and an outdoor whirlpool spa tub overlooking the neighboring vineyards and Mayacamus Mountains. After settling into their room, they enjoyed a leisurely stroll through the Harvest Inn's eight acres of beautiful gardens. "Just as you savor the aromas of superb wines, my nose appreciates fragrances. Just smell the wonderful perfumes emanating from the roses and fragrant fruit trees inhabiting this garden sanctuary," Stephanie said. "You bring up an interesting and intriguing comparison between wines and perfumes," Jason replied. "In the summer of 2004, I toured France sampling their finest wines and trying to educate my nose and palate. Toward the end of my tour I visited a perfumery in Grasse, a town in the foothills north of Cannes. I was amazed by the complexity of all the distillation processes involved in making a perfume extract. The rare scents of lavender, myrtle, jasmine, rose, orange blossoms and wild mimosa from flowers in the Grasse region were turned into an extraordinary spectrum of perfumes." "Do you like the perfume I'm wearing?" Stephanie asked. "Yes your perfume is very alluring," he replied. "The fragrances of perfumes are incredible, but I don't taste or drink perfumes like I do wine. Some perfumes are nearly 80% alcohol," he said. Stephanie laughed. She could only imagine how much it would the cost to buy the equivalent of a 750 ml. bottle of wine in her expensive perfume.

After their garden walk, they left to explore the nearby Schramsberg Vineyards with its excellent wines and incredible wine caves. Wandering down the long and deep wine caves was exciting. They could only imagine the labor involved in digging out these caves. "I think Chinese laborers originally hired to build railroads during the California Gold Rush were involved in digging out these caves," Jason said. "It must have been hard work," Stephanie replied. "I have heard that some of the descendants of these Chinese coolie cave diggers are now prominent business owners and entrepreneurs in San Francisco's Chinatown," he said. "I have a few Chinese friends," Stephanie replied. "They value education and hard work. In my opinion these are two of the most important ingredients that lead to success." "That's certainly true in my case," Jason said. "I received an excellent early education in option trading in Chicago. Now I enjoy competing with Valerie in La Jolla. We are both winners."

As they were sipping sparkling wine in the Schramsberg tasting room, Stephanie recalled Jason's explanation of the significance of the 1972 Toast of Peace between President Nixon and Chou Enlai. Mentioning that event to Jason, Stephanie remarked. "Wine has probably played an interesting role in world history." "Yes, it has," Jason replied. "As an example, did you know that Mohammed originally relished wine but then later banned its use? The Islamic nations largely prohibit the drinking of wine and alcohol of any kind. Think of the increase in the potential sales of wine and spirits if that were reversed." "You are the consummate businessman Jason. I suppose you would be buying call options on wine, beer and distillers if that were to occur," she said. "Of course I would. I'm pleased that you have insights into option trading."

After leaving Schramsberg Vineyards, they headed north to the Chateau Montelena Winery well known for its exceptional Cabernet Estate Sauvignon and excellent Napa Valley Chardonnay. Jason belonged to their wine club and had been a collector of their best Cabernet Sauvignon vintages for years.

There was an extraordinary feature to the Chateau Montelena property that Jason wanted to show Stephanie. It was Jade Lake. Jade Lake had been created on the winery property as a profound site of peace and tranquility decades ago. Walking across a wooden ramp to the Jade Lake Pavilion for lunch, Stephanie paused to take in a deep breath. She let it out slowly and repeating it, she completely relaxed. "Jason this is a hidden paradise. I could spend a lifetime here," she said. Jason was amused. He looked at the surrounding weeping willows bowing their heads down toward the lake and reflected on the scene. "It is beautiful and serene, but I would find it boring after just a few hours," he said. "Couldn't you rent out a space in the Chateau's upper floor to conduct your option trading on your computer," she asked. "When you were finished you could come down to the lake to unwind." "You forget that meeting with my clients and giving option seminars comprise an essential part of my business," he said. Stephanie face registered some dismay. Viewing the weeping willows she compared this site with the stately live oaks and large leafed maple trees situated on top of Pritchard hill at the winery they had recently visited. The contrasts were stark but they both shared a beauty that moved her deeply. Her romantic idealism differed greatly from Jason's pragmatic realism, but that didn't discourage her deep love for him. This magical trip had only intensified that love. She would look forward to many more trips in the future.

They left the peace and beauty of Jade Lake to enjoy Calistoga. Best known for its healing, mineral-rich geothermal hot springs they decided to partake in a mud and mineral bath, hot steam bath and salt water swim at one of the hot spring resorts. Rejuvenated they were appreciating the beautiful art work contained in the Lee Youngman Galleries and making purchases when Jason's cell phone buzzed. It was officer O' Reilly who announced. "We have arrested our hit and run suspect Mr. Gianelli. Could you both come down to the Napa Police Station to fill out witness statements regarding the accident?" he asked. "Of course," Jason said. "Congratulations on your excellent police investigation and capture. I would like to personally commend you to the Napa Police Chief if a meeting with him could be arranged." "Thank you Mr. Gianelli. I will see if I can set up a meeting with the chief," O'Reilly said. "I would appreciate your commendation." "Was the suspect surprised when you arrested him?" Jason asked. "He was shocked. His face registered disbelief and then it turned to anguish. As a defense attorney, he knows the penalties will be severe. I don't think he will be defending criminals for awhile, but he will meet quite a few in his prison," O'Reilly said. "Yes, his prison cell will not be quite as lavish as his home in Beverly Hills," Jason said.

After they disconnected, Jason shared the good news with Stephanie. "I'm so relieved," she said. "I was afraid he might escape detection." "O'Reilly wants to meet us at the Napa Police station this afternoon in order to sign witness papers," Jason said. "Well, let's go!" she exclaimed. "I want to stop at the Harvest Inn first to change and compose a commendation letter for O'Reilly and his team," Jason said. After penning a letter praising the professional demeanor and capabilities of Officer O'Reilly, they drove to the Napa Police Station. Soon after Jason and Stephanie had congratulated O'Reilly and signed the witness papers, they were ushered into the police chief's office. Jason lauded O'Reilly's actions and the police chief was genuinely pleased. "This is only the third time in my career as police chief that someone has taken the time to come to my office and directly praise the efforts of one of my officers. It's a rare event," he said. "I want to emphasize how much your commendation of Officer O'Reilly means to me. I received a similar commendation early in my career. I think it eventually helped me become the police chief." Jason handed him the commendation letter he had written. "Please have this letter placed into Officer O' Reilly's personnel file," Jason said. Reading the letter the chief smiled. "You have gone the distance Mr. Gianelli," he said. "When we viewed the mangled body of Melanie Brady our hearts were broken," Jason said. "We watched Brady Nelson wrap his arms around his dead wife and cry. It aroused in us a deep hatred for the man who killed her and left the scene. We want him brought to justice," he said. "Do you think he'll be convicted?" "Yes I'm sure he'll be convicted. The evidence against him is insurmountable. He may hire the best defense attorney in the country, but he will be convicted," the police chief replied. "We want to attend the trial. We want to testify against him and watch him squirm," Jason said. "The trial will probably not occur for at least six weeks and we're not sure where it will be held. His defense team will try to change the venue to best serve their client." "Wherever it is held we will be there," Jason said. Stephanie nodded her head in agreement. "May I have a look at him?" Jason asked. "Let me see if I can arrange that," the chief said. He picked up the phone and called the jail. In Napa the Board of Corrections not the Police department controlled the jail. Speaking to the head, Jason and Stephanie were cleared to view the prisoner.

As Jason faced the jailed prisoner, he snarled and said, "You coward. You wouldn't even stop to help the person you ran over." The prisoner was heavy set and had ruddy cheeks. His eyes were cold and penetrating. He had a smirk on his face. It didn't portray any remorse. He just stared at Jason with steely eyes and didn't utter a word. Although he knew he would face a fine and prison term, he was hoping for only two years in prison. After he was released, he would resume his law practice and completely forget the anguish his drunken actions had provoked. He could live with his conscience. Jason perceived the unfeeling nature of this man and he hated him even more. Jason had to restrain himself. He wanted to spit in his face, but he only glared back and said. "Remember my face. I will testify against you during your trial. I watched you murder an innocent woman and then leave the scene. You are despicable." The prisoner only smiled and turned away from Jason. He was ruthless and hardened like the criminals he defended. Jason felt rage in his heart, but he could only turn around and leave the jail. Stephanie had waited outside. She didn't want to see the killer. In that way she could avoid visualizing his face in a nightmare.

Of course Jason appeared to be so heroic and highly principled in his statements to the police chief. He appeared to champion justice. He portrayed righteous indignation when he verbally accosted Richard Kramer in the jail. Richard Kramer had disregarded the injuries and agony he caused when he ran over Melanie Nelson and their unborn child. Jason too was ruthless and unfeeling in his dealings with Valerie and his co-workers. In reality Jason was a two faced snake filled with poisonous venom. He would willingly strike out at anyone who stood in his way. Jason Gianelli and Richard Kramer were in many ways clones.

After they left the jail, they relaxed and enjoyed a delicious meal at the famous Cole's Chop House in Napa.

Returning to the events of the day Stephanie remarked. "I've experienced such a wide swing in my emotions today. I felt such peace at Jade Lake. With the capture of Melanie's killer my emotions were completely twisted. I felt a surge of hate toward him," she said. "We can't let this fiend destroy our vacation," Jason said. "It's so hard to purge him from my mind," Stephanie said. "I'm glad I didn't see him. It's easier to just have a vision of a blank face in front of me."

"I've arranged for a private masseuse to help you relax tonight in our suite," Jason said. "Just try to empty anger out of your mind and focus completely on your body as she gives you a massage." "I'll try Jason," she said. "It won't be easy, but I'll try."

She was able to completely let go and relax back in their room. "How does it feel, Stephanie?" Jason asked as the masseuse was plying her body. "I think I'm in heaven," she said. Jason's sudden vision of Stephanie entering heaven startled him. Would he be able to join her there?

Later that night they made love with such intensity they were released from the cares of the day. The killer was behind bars and they were glad. They soon fell into a deep and refreshing sleep.

# Chapter 27

AFTER A LEISURELY stroll around the gardens at the Harvest Inn, they ate breakfast and planned their day. Jason suggested they take the aerial tram up the hill to the Sterling Vineyards. The views going up in the tram of gardens and ponds were breathtaking. Following the self-guided wine tour they stopped to enjoy the reserve and VIP tastings. From the upper deck patio they surveyed the Napa Valley vistas below them. "It's so beautiful," Stephanie said. "I agree," Jason said. "We are so fortunate to live in the USA. The freedoms we enjoy are incredible. They allow everyone to pursue an endless number of opportunities. No one has to remain in a rut. You do have to stretch your imagination, educate yourself in the field of your dreams, and pursue it with a passion." "Is that what you've done Jason?" she asked. "Yes, my occupation is thrilling and challenging. I found the Chicago Option Pits exhilarating. I relished every day I served on the options floor," he said. "Why did you leave then?" Stephanie asked. "Getting up at 4 AM during the cold winter months in Chicago was horrible. When the opportunity to trade options while living in La Jolla presented itself, I grabbed it. I still relish my everyday option trading. I lead a very exciting and gratifying life in a much warmer climate. You have been the special prize that also came with the move Stephanie," he said. She let out a laugh. "That's a real stretch! Yes, we started dating 21 years after you left Chicago!" "That's called a delayed bonus," Jason said.

He was so enthusiastic and vibrant. She loved being with him. Briefly she thought of Valerie who was not at all enthralled with Jason. In fact she knew how much Valerie disliked him and that disturbed her. She so wished they could become friends as they were the two most important people in her life. She wondered how she could become a conduit toward resolving their differences. Unfortunately, no strategy entered her mind.

"Let's go to the The Culinary Institute of America at Greystone," Jason said. "I've made reservations for a cooking demonstration. I think you'll enjoy it." "I'd love to do that," she said. "Let's go."

The live cooking class was held in a large theater and performed by some of the school's renowned chef-instructors. It was fabulous. Afterwards Stephanie tried to sign up for a gourmet cooking class later in the year but all the places had been reserved. "I'll have to make a reservation for the gourmet cooking class well in advance of our return trip to Napa Valley, Jason." "Are you sure you want to come back to Napa?" he asked. "Absolutely, this has been the best trip I've ever taken in my life."

Jason's smile radiated his pleasure. He wanted so much to please her. "I promise to bring you back to Napa Valley next year. We can only sample a small portion of Napa Valley in this one week birthday tour," he said.

They continued their exploration of the Culinary Institute. The multiple components of the historic tour, the museum, herb garden and view of the teaching kitchen were impressive. Jason paused in front of the famous center for professional wine studies. "I've dreamed of taking classes on wine instruction here someday," he said. He knew deep in his heart that it wouldn't happen. He was too addicted to his option trading. In his warped but efficient mind he thought that he couldn't afford to take the time off. Perhaps an online computer course would suffice instead. He knew that would be a poor substitute.

Option trading was Jason's passion. He enjoyed his intense investment rivalry with Valerie. It served to motivate him to generate the highest income in the Kaplan firm even if it meant luring clients away from her and other co-workers. Being the premier investment advisor in the firm took precedence over everything and everyone in his life. Perhaps that even included Stephanie, he mused. That was a disquieting thought. Yes, this trip had intensified his love for Stephanie, but it had not dampened his perverse need to surpass Valerie as an investment advisor. Valerie probably hated him for his devious tactics in taking clients away from her. When Dr. and

Mrs. Friedman defected to him she was furious. He didn't care what she thought. He would do whatever it took to exceed her investment returns and her commission income. It allowed him to send even more money to his mother. She needed it. His mother was proud of him and that was important to Jason. He would continue to hide his ruthless nature from Stephanie. It would only disturb her.

Stephanie purchased both an Italian and Gourmet cookbook in the Spice Islands Marketplace. She wanted to impress Jason with her cooking skills. Someday she hoped Jason would propose marriage. Her heart longed deeply for that magical day. It was her most precious dream. It was a yearning she could not suppress. Nor did she try!

Finally it was time for their dinner reservation in the Wine Spectator Greystone Restaurant. Jason had a special treat in store for Stephanie. He had arranged for the purchase of a Vintage 1987 Chateau Montelena Estate Cabernet Sauvignon to accompany their appetizing food. One of the leading wine critics gave it a rating of 98 points. "I judge a wine based upon how much it pleases my own individual nose and palate," Jason said. "For me this is a superb vintage. The flavors are exquisite and the finish is incredible. Notice how long the wine lasts in the back of your throat and after you swallow it." Stephanie was not an expert in wine tasting. "You appreciate the subtleties of wine. I'm just a novice. Please continue to teach me about wines after we return to La Jolla." "I promise to do that," he replied. "I have a wine cellar full of outstanding vintages in my home. Now that you've had some instruction in wine tasting you will appreciate drinking them with me even more than in the past."

They enjoyed their delicious meal and the incredible wine. This was what successful option trading was all about, Jason thought. Being able to afford the best food, wine and accommodations with the woman he loved made his occupation rewarding. He reveled over the thought that his computer option trades were paying for this entire trip! He led a charmed life and he wanted to enjoy it for decades to come!

Jason experienced some stomach discomfort during the meal. "What's wrong, Jason?" Stephanie asked as they left the restaurant. "I think my ulcer is acting up again," he replied. "We could try to get an antacid at a drug store if one is open," she replied. "It's already better," he said. "It's nothing serious."

The next morning they departed Napa to drive to San Jose and catch their flight to San Diego. It had been a memorable trip. "Jason when can we return to the Napa Valley?" she asked shortly after leaving the Harvest Inn. He laughed. "We haven't even left Napa Valley. Are you that eager for a return trip?" he asked. "Yes I am. This has been far and away the best vacation I've ever had. You've made it so special. I want you to know how much I appreciate what you've done for me," she added. "For us you mean," he said. "Sharing these experiences together with you has made the trip special for me too. Without you I would have found this trip lonely and rather uninteresting. It's the magic of our love for one another enjoyed in an idyllic location that made this trip exceptional," he said. She was hoping he would say that. She felt deep in her heart that she wanted to spend the rest of her life with him. "Well, let's just say that I would like to share a re-peat trip to the Napa Valley with you. I will leave it up to you to plan it. I will drop everything to go with you again."

# Chapter 28

WITH DR. FRIEDMAN'S influence it had taken Valerie only one week to get a cardiology appointment with Dr. Melissa Chang in the La Jolla Center for Integrative Medicine. Dr. Friedman had urged Valerie to explore the Center's programs in order to gain insights into her heart disease. He suspected the adverse effects of stress especially anger, hostility and depression were playing a significant role in producing her coronary heart disease.

Dr. Chang greeted Valerie and said. "Mrs. Goldin, Dr. Friedman has discussed with me his reasons for referring you to me. He's been concerned over your stress levels as they relate to your heart condition. What are your stress issues?" she asked. "I operate in the world of investments and my clients expect me to make money for them," Valerie replied. "From what he told me you've been very successful in doing that over a period of 24 years. There must be more to it than that," she said.

Valerie decided to directly divulge her problem. "I have a very toxic relationship with one of my investment advisor co-workers, Jason Gianelli. I was impressed by his skill in employing option strategies when we both joined the Kaplan Investment Services firm in 1986. I tried to become his friend and asked him to teach me some of his option strategies. He was reluctant to share his insights with me. Gradually he began to steal my clients and downplay my investment results. Naturally I became annoyed. He started to brag about his option strategies and to criticize my investment methods behind my back. My anger naturally began to smolder and I grew to genuinely dislike him." "Did this dislike evolve over a matter of years?" Dr. Chang asked. "Yes, it gradually worsened over a period of several years. When I lost money on stocks in the banking and home building sectors in 2008, he broadcasted this to participants in his option seminars. Several more of my clients transferred their assets over to him." "Does he produce a decent investment return for his clients?" Dr. Chang asked. "Yes, he is extremely adept in producing incredibly high returns. He touts his superior results in his weekly option seminars. His clients share his spectacular returns with others in the investment community. This has led to the further exodus of several of my major clients and those of my co-workers to Jason. I'm frustrated and angry over his actions and envious of his success. Can you help me?" Valerie asked. "Yes, I think I can along with the help of some of my colleagues."

"Is Mr. Gianelli the main cause of your stress or are there other people or factors involved?" she asked. "No, Mr. Gianelli has been the major source of my underlying stress. He seems to delight in frustrating me. I have grown to actually hate him for creating so much turmoil in my life," she said. "Hate is a very strong word Mrs. Goldin. Do you actually hate him?" "Yes I do Doctor Chang. I hate him. He has upset me so many times and in so many ways that I bristle every time I see him. He seems to take a perverse pleasure in causing me distress. He tried recently to steal my largest investment account," she said. "I assume that was Dr. Friedman's account," Dr. Chang replied. "He relayed that story to me. I was shocked by the brazen and secretive nature of Mr. Gianelli's actions while you were out of the office recovering from your knee surgery and heart problem. He does appear to be rather reprehensible on the surface. Is that an accurate assessment?" she asked. "Yes, but Jason has another side to him that is supposedly attractive. He is dating my closest friend and an investment client, Stephanie Shea. She lost her much older husband to colon cancer five years ago. She's been dating Jason for the past three years and keeps telling me how wonderful he is. That may be true in her life, but he has a horrible way of dealing with his co-workers. In fact he was responsible for the suicide death of one of them, John Davenport." "How did he cause Mr. Davenport's suicide?" Dr Chang asked. "Jason had taken away several of John's clients through his option seminars. When John became depressed and an alcoholic over it, several of us tried to help him, but not Jason. Finally John's largest client defected to Jason. Soon after that John became more despondent and committed suicide by hanging himself. Laura, his wife, found him dangling from a rope around his neck in their garage. He had apparently climbed up a ladder and tied the rope to a garage rafter. Then he must have tied it around his neck and jumped off the ladder. It was a horrifying experience for Laura and her two young children. We were all stunned at the office, but not Jason. He didn't even attend the funeral." "But surely he expressed some sympathy," Dr. Chang said. "Not at all," Valerie replied. "He signed the condolence office card reluctantly. He didn't contribute a cent to the Davenport office relief fund. Everyone else in the office contributed and some were very generous. Does that give you a better picture of my rival?" she asked. Dr. Chang was appalled. "Is he actually that despicable and unfeeling?" she replied. "Except in his relationship with Stephanie and his clients, he is a terrible and malicious man. I can't emphasize how much I disrespect and hate him," Valerie said.

Dr. Chang was stunned by the virulence contained in Valerie's voice. "I'll refer you to one of our experts in the field of meditation to see if she can help allay some of your distress," she said. "You will need to learn relaxation techniques. Yoga and progressive muscle contraction and release methods will potentially help you too. There are many other programs in our center that will help you make important changes in dealing with the stress invoked by Jason Gianelli." "I will be so grateful if your program resolves some of the stress in my life," Valerie said. "I am completely aware of your coronary artery anatomy and stent location," Dr. Chang said. "The structural aspects of your heart condition have been successfully addressed. We will focus on the stress related issues contributing to your premature heart disease. The program we develop for you will hopefully help prevent further progression of your coronary heart disease."

"I will give you a number of handouts today. Each one contains a one page summary of each individual program and its major purpose. They also include such things as the time it's offered, the nature and benefits of the program, the location and cost. I suggest you look them over and plan to sample the ones you find interesting and useful." "I'll study them carefully," Valerie said. "I would urge you to sign up for the first level swim class," Dr.

Chang said. "It's held in our beautiful outdoor pool which overlooks the Pacific Ocean three days a week starting at one pm. I think it will help relieve some of your stress."

"I think swimming may provide me with an outlet for my exercise needs," Valerie said. "Not being able to play tennis has been very frustrating." "Besides swimming I would like you sample the Qigong Meditation seated class. Later on when your knee is stronger you may want to add Tai Chi. For now just explore what's available. Sample those programs you find appealing and return to see me in three weeks. Working together I think we can design a personalized and unique program especially designed to deal with your anger and frustration."

"I have taken the liberty to schedule a few consultation appointments for you with some of our instructors. I hope you can make them," Dr. Chang said. "Engaging in your program has become my number one priority," Valerie said. "I'll make the consultation appointments. In addition I'll sign up for the one pm swimming class and sample the programs available to me. I'm eager to get started. It seems both my heart and I hunger for a change!"

# Chapter 29

VALERIE LEFT DR. Chang's office bolstered by a ray of hope. She reviewed the consultations with the practitioners of stress reduction. She noticed there was also a dietary consultation. I suppose they will want me to become a vegetarian too she thought. Later on in the program she was scheduled to see an exercise physiologist. Dr. Chang had recommended the progressive swimming program be started as soon as possible. That was preferred over weight bearing exercises because of her recent total right knee replacement.

Valerie was impressed. She hadn't thought of swimming. It was such a logical choice. She berated herself for being so blinded by her hostility toward Jason. The importance of initiating a lifestyle modification program was paramount in her life. Perhaps she could eventually escape the underlying distress Jason was causing her. For the first time in years she felt a surge of hope.

At home that evening Valerie started to pet her adorable dog Sasha. It was an action that always helped her relax. Sasha was wagging her tail enjoying Valerie's attention.

Valerie began to review with Charles the various handouts Dr. Chang had given her earlier that day. "What a wide range of programs," she said. Charles laughed. "You may have to quit your job if you want to attend all of them," he said. "No I'll be very selective. I'll take a sample class and see if it appeals to me. I want to start slowly. I don't want to jeopardize my investment returns and short change my clients. Jason would take advantage of me if I did that. I'm going to become an active member of the La Jolla Center for Integrative Medicine. Some of these programs should help reduce the anger and hostility I feel toward Jason."

Charles looked pleased. He caught a glimmer of hope in Valerie's eyes as he watched her review the various programs. He yearned for the day when she could control her animosity toward Jason. "Of course I'll have to discuss this with Robert Kaplan before I embark on any program," she said. "I'll meet with him tomorrow morning to review the tentative swimming schedule." Charles looked over Valerie's proposed one pm swimming schedule and nodded approvingly. "This seems to be a reasonable way to start. I think Robert will approve of the swimming program. He wants you to reduce your stress too," he said. "He has agonized over the way Jason has been treating you and so have I." Valerie gave Charles a hug. "I love you Charles. Thanks for supporting me."

# Chapter 30

VALERIE WAS APPREHENSIVE when she met with Robert Kaplan the next morning. He served as her investment mentor during her early years with his firm. He had educated her in conservative investment principles and strategies. Moreover he was a highly principled man who stressed the importance of honesty and integrity in dealing with clients.

Valerie had grown up in a loving and generous family. She had always tried to please her parents. They had encouraged her to be inquisitive and to pursue a variety of interests as she matured. Her father had retired as a successful executive engineer and her mother as a philosophy professor. When Valerie achieved academic and athletic prominence at Stanford they were naturally proud of her. Now she was also seeking approval from Robert Kaplan. She respected him and wanted to please him too. Valerie loved her parents. She genuinely liked Robert Kaplan. She wondered what he would think of the La Jolla Center for Integrative Medicine programs.

After Robert reviewed the swimming program and some of the sample programs Valerie had selected as possible additions, he said. "These are incredible programs Valerie. I wholeheartedly support you in initiating them." "I think I can still fit my clients into various time frames during the week," Valerie said. "After watching you react to Jason during your welcoming back office party, I think this type of training will be of tremendous benefit for you." "Was I that bad Robert?" she asked. "You appeared to be devastated by Jason's actions. Look at what subsequently happened. You developed a serious heart rhythm disturbance that could have led to a stroke.

Stress reduction should become your number one priority. I want you to enter this program." "Thank you Robert." Her face beamed with satisfaction and pleasure. "Your support is very important to me."

She left his office and immediately called Charles. "Robert has given me the green light to engage in the La Jolla Center for Integrative Medicine programs. In fact he almost ordered me to do it!" she exclaimed. "That's terrific. When will you start?" he asked. "Next Monday."

She returned to her office grateful for the support important people in her life were giving her. She vowed to conquer her malignant relationship with Jason. He could still upset her, but she hoped to be able to handle it better. The Friedmans had entrusted $6 million dollars to her and she set out to make it grow.

Turning on her VectorVest computer program she reviewed her client accounts. Her eyes glowed as she observed how much the Friedman's assets had already grown through her VectorVest based stock selections. VectorVest, Inc. had been created and founded by a brilliant mathematician and engineer named Bart DiLiddo, PhD. She had been successfully using the VectorVest stock analysis service since 1998. She wanted to currently identify and buy safe, undervalued stocks with consistent, predictable and growing earnings. As a prudent investor, Valerie had heeded the VectorVest confirmed market up call issued on March 26, 2009. She had proceeded to aggressively buy top rated VST graded stocks and had been achieving excellent investment returns. She found the logic underlying the VectorVest program intriguing.

VectorVest calculates a proprietary indicator called relative value or RV which identifies long term price appreciation potential. On a scale of 0.00 to 2.00 stocks with a RV greater than 1.00 should outperform the AAA corporate bond over the next three years. She preferred to buy undervalued stocks in a rising stock market. Using safety or RS with other proprietary indicators such as relative timing or RT had been providing her clients with excellent investment gains with lower downside risk. Encouraged by improving corporate earnings, the low rate investment environment being promulgated by the Federal Reserve Board and the relatively low inflation rates, Valerie was continuing to use VectorVest to identify potential stock picks.

After an early 2010 "flash crash", the bull market had resumed in the summer of 2010 and she wanted to take advantage of it. Clicking on the views tab she scrolled down to the Strategy of the Week. She always found the dissertations by Dr. DiLiddo insightful. She had compiled a folder containing strategies for finding stocks to buy long in upturns dating back to April 8, 2004. If used judiciously, the strategies employed could produce rather dramatic results. She longed to beat out Jason in her annualized return this year. It was difficult to compete against his option trading using a margin account. Perhaps she could use VectorVest's option trading techniques to invest some of their own personal money. She would discuss that with Charles tonight. The thought excited her.

# Chapter 31

VALERIE HAD ALREADY been swimming for three days a week when she had her follow up appointment with Dr. Chang. "Thank you for suggesting the swimming program Dr Chang," Valerie said. "I'm feeling much stronger and also more relaxed." "Are you ready to move into some stress reduction classes Valerie?" Dr. Chang asked. "Yes I'm ready. I've attended several different sessions and I've chosen to attend Qigong and Kundalini Yoga classes," Valerie replied. "I was impressed by your endorsement of Qigong during our first meeting. I think it will be very helpful in reducing my stress. I had never heard of Kundalini Yoga but I was very impressed by the instructor." "She's an outstanding teacher," Dr. Chang said. "Yes, she is. I'd heard about the benefits of chanting a mantra in the past, but always laughed over it. When I told Charles I had selected a mantra, he gave me a quizzical look like I was becoming a freak. He even made fun of me when I started to chant. Now he is observing that I have more energy and vitality and he's surprised." "You will find chanting your mantra especially helpful during stressful situations," Dr. Chang said. "The real test will come when I have a new conflict with Jason," Valerie replied. "I haven't had any clashes with him over the past two weeks so I'm not sure how effective my yoga techniques will be when one of our disastrous encounters explodes in my face." "Has anything helped in the past?" Dr. Chang asked. "No, nothing has helped. Let's see if the techniques I'm learning in these two classes help me deal with my nemesis when a new battle rages."

Dr. Chang could feel the impact of Valerie's animosity toward Mr. Gianelli. It was palpable. Valerie's emotions of anger and hostility were very real and substantial. Dr. Chang realized that Valerie would have to master stress reduction techniques before she would be successful in even partially modifying her reactions to Mr. Gianelli. This was going to be a challenge she thought. "Are there any other aspects of our center that you would like to explore?" Dr Chang asked. "Yes I would like to enroll in the La Jolla Life Improvement Center. I could use a personal trainer," Valerie said. "Well let's work out a schedule for you to include the Life Improvement Center and see what evolves over the next two weeks at which time I would like to see you back in my office," Dr. Chang said.

When the schedule was completed Valerie looked at it and frowned. The somber look on her face revealed her concern. "I hope I can keep my investment clients satisfied," she said. "I'll be out of the office for more time than I can probably afford. Jason will probably take advantage of my absence to steal more of my clients." "You can always cut back on this schedule should that occur Valerie," Dr. Chang said. "By then it may be too late. Once Jason gets his hooks into a client, it's almost impossible to win that client back," Valerie said. "Is he that persuasive?" Dr. Chang asked. "He can be both persuasive and charming. He is also extremely effective in generating impressive investment returns. As long as that persists, clients will stay with him," Valerie said. "He must make some investment mistakes," Dr. Chang said. "He does make mistakes, but not very many. He is also adept at cutting his losses swiftly," Valerie said. "He just has an uncanny ability to make exceptional option trades. I can't successfully compete with his returns. All I can do is maintain a steady investment return for my clients with a much more acceptable risk profile." "What would it take to make him more acceptable?" Dr. Chang asked.

"If he would share some of his current option trades with the rest of us in the office, we would find him more acceptable as a co-worker. Unfortunately he is very secretive. He won't share any useful investment advice with us," Valerie said. "I thought he gave option seminars at your firm. Shouldn't they help you make profitable trades?" Dr. Chang asked. "In his option seminars he only refers to past option trades that are no longer pertinent. Then he warns people not to employ them because they

are outdated and potentially dangerous. You can't obtain his current thinking unless you are willing to become one of his clients. Some of the money
managers in our firm have actually turned over their personal money to him
to invest. It's the only way to obtain insights into his current option plays.
Even if I had that information I would be uncomfortable initiating any of
his current option positions. I wouldn't know when to exit the trades," she
said. "He is a very clever and yet a devious opponent. I continue to despise
him. I just can't help feeling that way for all the things he's done to me."
"You will have to gain better control over your emotions," Dr. Chang remarked. "Otherwise you'll continue to have stress placed on your heart. I
don't want you to have another heart attack," she said. "I don't want a
stroke either," Valerie replied. "Just immerse yourself into our stress management techniques and employ them whenever he upsets you." "I'll try,"
Valerie said.

Dr. Chang had not realized how talented Jason Gianelli was in the
field of money managers. He was also cunning in his relationships with
people. The way he had cleverly orchestrated his strategy to obtain Dr.
Friedman's account from Valerie was rather brilliant she thought. She
found his duplicity, however, abhorrent. Dr. Chang tried to measure her
own reactions to his actions and also experienced some anger. She could
now understand the intensity of Valerie's distrust and dislike of Mr.
Gianelli. To help Valerie control her hostile reactions toward Mr. Gianelli
would become one her greatest challenges. She would try her best to help
Valerie, but it wasn't going to be easy.

# Chapter 32

VALERIE WAS ENCOURAGED but still frustrated when she returned to her office. She turned on her computer and returned to VectorVest in search of stocks to bolster her clients' investment returns. From the home page she clicked on the Unisearch tool and scrolled down to the search-prudent envelope. She had used stock selections from Chappell's Champs on many occasions in the past with excellent results. She found the criteria used in Chappell's Champs to be very compelling. First the stocks had to be ranked in the top 100 based upon a combination of value, safety and timing. This was the proprietary formula that was key to the VectorVest program and abbreviated to VST. Next over 100,000 shares per day had to be traded in order to provide the needed liquidity. It was the combination of a high VST, the highest comfort index and the highest earnings per share that made the search so powerful. She clicked on the run search and the top 20 stocks meeting those criteria popped up on her computer screen. She critically analyzed multiple additional parameters before adding a stock into her clients' portfolios.

Since the broad market was still in an uptrend, she felt more confident in buying stocks. She also employed sell criteria. She might decide on taking profits if the stock rose 40 to 50 percent. On the other hand she used stop loss orders to limit losses. VectorVest was a much more sophisticated stock analysis service than others she had employed. There were many nuances Valerie had discovered in using VectorVest successfully over the years. She had not been surprised when Dr. and Mrs. Friedman told her about losing money during a rising market in 2009. Becoming an expert in any field of endeavor took years of study. That was true in surgery, law, engineering, computer science and a broad range of academic disciplines. It was also true in money management. Finding and employing the best tools to achieve success was critical in reaching the top of any chosen field of endeavor.

Valerie had the advantage of studying under excellent professors at Stanford both as an undergraduate and graduate student. They had instilled in her the importance of continuing the quest for knowledge and discovery upon graduation. When she discovered Dr. Bart DiLiddo, PhD, the editor and founder of VectorVest, she was richly rewarded both financially and intellectually. She had embraced his guidance on strategy and market timing. Her investment results were enviable and largely due to his influence in discovering the mathematics and science behind investment decisions.

She took a break and stepped out of her office to access the lobby coffee machine. Before she returned to her office she happened to notice Jason Gianelli delivering an option training session in the office conference room. He was moving back and forth in front of an easel plotting graphs and adding figures. He certainly had an impressive profile and an engaging smile she thought. Jason collected amusing stories, anecdotes, and jokes which he would intersperse into his seminars. He must have just told one because everyone suddenly started to laugh. He could coax laughter out of anyone.

The audience seemed to be captivated by Jason. In surveying those in attendance she suddenly spotted Barry Greenberg and her heart started to race. Barry was one of the brightest computer scientists working at the local San Diego large chip company with her husband Charles. He was responsible for obtaining more than 20 important patents for the company and was now one of the vice presidents. He was also one of Valerie's major clients. She felt a sense of betrayal as she watched Barry's smile as he listened to Jason's insights. It was happening again. Jason was trying to lure another one of her clients away from her. As anger began to overcome her, she thought of Dr. Chang, Qigong and Kundalini Yoga. She hurried back into her office and began to meditate employing her own personal mantra. She closed her eyes and began to take slow deep breaths. To her dismay it wasn't working. A vision of Jason's smiling face kept appearing in her mind.

She tried desperately to purge his image from her conscious with only partial success. If only she could experience love and benevolence she thought. As she continued, she briefly felt some relief. Unfortunately it was superseded by feelings of animosity and hostility. She persisted in applying her newly discovered stress reduction techniques. Slowly a modicum of inner harmony emerged. It was a start.

# Chapter 33

VALERIE WAS ENJOYING a glass of Cabernet Sauvignon with Charles on their outdoor patio when the image of a smiling Barry Greenberg entered her mind. "Charles, I saw Barry Greenberg today. He was attending one of Jason's option seminars. His face registered genuine interest and he was smiling," she said. "That wouldn't surprise me. Barry is a highly regarded mathematician and computer scientist. He grasps mathematical principles that are way over my head. We were in the same PhD computer science program at the University of California San Diego, but he was simultaneously taking higher mathematics classes. He obtained a master's degree in mathematics and one year later his PhD in computer science. The math department tried to hire him as a professor while he was still a graduate student. If anyone could excel in option trading I think it would be Barry," he said. "In fact, if he put his mind to it I would wager he could produce higher returns than your competitor Jason Gianelli." Valerie's heart sank. A look of dismay crossed her face. "That means he will switch a good portion of his account with me to Jason," Valerie replied. "Not necessarily," Charles responded. "I think Barry will dabble in option trading just for the challenge. He's told me that he appreciates the fact that you manage his investment account. He said that he is much too busy to involve himself in stock and bond investing." "I hope you're right," Valerie replied. "The anger that welled up in me when I saw Barry in Jason's option session was rather overwhelming. My stress reduction techniques were only minimally effective in controlling my distress." "Valerie, you are a relative neophyte in using Qigong and Kundalini Yoga to combat stressful situations. Give them more time."

In reality petting Sasha gave Valerie more stress relief than drinking wine. Sasha, her Yorkshire terrier had jumped into Valerie's lap and was snuggling up to her looking lovingly into Valerie's eyes. Valerie hugged Sasha and a warm glow of satisfaction came over her. Those who love dogs know exactly how she felt. It was a feeling that you couldn't readily explain. But it was real and it was soothing. She loved Sasha with all her heart.

Competing with Jason was taking its toll. "I've been competing with Jason for the last 24 years. It's time for a change. I'm beginning to accept myself for my own unique qualities. Perhaps I can accept Jason's for his qualities too. I'm afraid if I don't I will just remain frustrated and unhappy," she said. Charles was excited. His eyes brightened as he smiled. "I think you've gained some important insights from your instructors in Integrative Medicine," he said. "Yes, I have. I'm on a slow path toward recovery. In general I'm happier and more content than I've been in years. I'm embracing an attitude of gratefulness rather than resentment. Beside that I'm taking better care of myself. I still haven't forgiven Jason for all the stress he's produced in my life."

Charles refilled her glass with more Cabernet Sauvignon. "Maybe this wine will help to ease your stress," he said. "Well I'm not the only person experiencing stress," she replied. "Our group sessions have helped me realize the extent of anxiety present in lives of many others not just mine. We're trying to help one another improve our relationships with people in general and especially with ourselves.

"What other insights have you gleaned from your Integrative Medicine classes so far Valerie?" Charles asked. "Well I'm finally realizing that I can determine my own personal reactions to stressful situations. It's up to me to modify my emotional reactions. I've allowed Jason to frustrate and enrage me," she said. "That has to change." "He's been a very detrimental factor in your life and your health. I wish it would stop," Charles replied. "I may be able to at least modify it. I came across a remarkable story about a Jewish psychiatrist who was a prisoner in a Nazi death camp," Valerie said. "He was able to decide within himself how the horrible treatment he was experiencing was going to affect him. He realized that he had the power to choose his own personal response to despicable treatment." "What would he do?" Charles asked. "He knew his Nazi prison guards had more liberty, but he conjectured that he had in essence more freedom to chose his own response to their actions." "What do you mean?" Charles asked. "He searched for meaning in his suffering and more dignity in his personal existence," she said. "How did he accomplish that?" Charles asked. "He realized that between a stimulus and response he had the freedom to choose his own personal reaction," she said. "That's an incredibly powerful insight. For example when Jason creates havoc in my life, I will try to use my imagination and personal strength to choose a more tranquil response and not react in anger." "I think that's a real stretch," Charles said. "That's not a normal response." "Of course it isn't. But that's why it's so powerful. It converts a spontaneous negative response into a more reflective positive response."

"The real test will come over my ability to generate forgiveness for Jason's egregious actions," she said. "That will entail a rather radical paradigm shift on your part," Charles said. "Do you actually think you're capable of responding in that fashion?" "I'm going to try. I want to convert my negative reactions to Jason into more positive emotional responses. I'm not even close to accomplishing that yet, but I am encouraged by my progress. If I can free myself from the malignant effects Jason creates in my life, I will be much happier," she said. "You will be healthier too" Charles replied. "We now know that feelings of hate and hostility adversely affect the heart. I don't want you back in the hospital requiring an additional stent." "You're right," she said. "I want my heart to be happy too. In fact I want to develop a better sense of humor. I've become much too serious. Will you help me laugh and enjoy my life more?" Charles face brightened. His eyes widened and he broke into a broad grin. "I guess we could go to some movies to watch comedies. I could always buy you some good joke books." Charles realized that Valerie had indeed become too serious. She wasn't enjoying life. Jason's actions were taking a toll. "I'll try to make you laugh more," he said. But he was a serious computer scientist himself. His sense of humor wasn't well developed either. He was skilled in developing computer chips, but inept in creating laughter.

"I finally have access to a personalized stress reduction program and I intend to utilize it to my fullest ability. I've resolved to change my lifestyle and my reaction pathways," Valerie said. Charles thought those were lofty goals, but did she have the ability to reach them? He was doubtful. Jason's blatant tactics to steal Valerie's clients and downplay her investment strategies had deeply affected her over the course of 24 years. She was still not coping very well. "Exactly how are you going to accomplish that change?" Charles asked. "Whenever I encounter stress I will utilize a relaxation technique to counter it. Let's see what happens over the ensuing months," she said. "I've embarked upon a program designed to cause a mental, emotional and physical transformation. I intend to stay on course until that healthy transformation occurs." Charles looked at her with love in his eyes. She was critical to his happiness. He would welcome the transformation should it occur. He had watched Valerie struggle over the disappointments caused by client defections to Jason. He despised Jason's actions They had to be resolved.

# Chapter 34

THE TRIAL OF Richard Kramer had been moved to Los Angeles at the request of his defense attorney. He claimed there had been too much publicity in Napa and the surrounding areas for his client to obtain a fair trial in northern California. Jason and Stephanie had left Napa Valley six weeks earlier. Now the trial was about to start. The jury had been selected and they were seated in the jury box, seven men and five women.

The first witness was called to the stand. Officer O'Reilly appeared impressive dressed in his police uniform. He looked very professional. His demeanor was serious and his answers to questions were crisp. After taking the oath to tell the truth, the whole truth, and nothing but the truth so help me God, the prosecutor began his questioning.

"Please state your full name," he said. "Robert J. O'Reilly, sir," he replied. "What is your occupation?" "I am a Napa California police officer." "On September 13, 2010 were you summoned to a bicycle accident on the Silverado Trail several miles north of Napa?" "Yes sir," he said. "Will you describe what you observed?" "After I received a call from a Mr. Jason Gianelli at approximately 12:30 PM on that date, I drove to the scene and observed the mangled body of a young woman and her bicycle off to the right side of the road. The medics had just arrived ahead of me and had pronounced her dead," he said. "Had anyone observed the accident?" the prosecutor asked. "Yes, Mr. Jason Gianalli and Mrs. Stephanie Shea stepped forward and testified that they had witnessed the collision," he said. "Did they identify the driver who hit the victim?" he asked. "No they were not able to identify the driver. They said that the driver had sped away from the scene driving north on the Silverado Trail at a high rate of speed," he responded. "Did they notice the manufacturer of the car or the license number?" he asked. "They only described the car as being a white sedan and they were unable to read the license plate number," he responded. "What did you do next?" he asked. "I dispatched an all out alert to apprehend a white sedan that was last heading north on the Silverado Trail at approximately 12:30 pm. Unfortunately they were unable to find the car or the hit and run driver," he added.

"What did you do next?" he asked. "I interviewed the distraught husband, Mr. Brady Nelson who was clutching his dead wife and sobbing." "And what did he say?" "He told me that he and his wife were leisurely riding their bikes in the right hand bike lane when the sedan smashed into his wife," O'Reilly said. "Was he struck too?" "No he wasn't. He said the car barely missed him as it swerved back out of the bike lane into the northbound lane of the highway." "Was his wife in the bike lane?" "Yes she was. He said they were careful to stay well into the right bike lane which is also rather wide on the Silverado Trail. He said that he was riding his bike about five yards in front of his wife when the accident occurred."

Brady Nelson had started to sob as the story unfolded. All eyes from the jury turned and focused on him. He could not be consoled and just kept crying. Tears welled up in the eyes of all five of the women jurors. Some of the men in the jury seemed moved too. They could only imagine what he was feeling. "You mentioned that the wife was dead. Was anyone else hurt Officer O'Reilly?" "Well, yes. Mr. Brady told me that his wife was pregnant with their three month old unborn son. He died in the crash too." A gasp arose from the jury box. One woman, cried out. "Oh no." Then the whole courtroom went silent except for the muffled cries coming from Brady Nelson.

"How did you find the suspect Officer O'Reilly?" he asked. "We traced the damaged sedan to an auto repair shop in Santa Rosa, California and we apprehended him three days later." "How did you know it was his car?" he asked. "I had interviewed the bartender at the Clarion Napa Valley Winery which is located about one mile south of the scene of the accident. Jason Gianelli had observed the sedan barreling out of the Clarion driveway just in front of them as they were driving north on the Silverado Trail. They described the car as swerving half way into the south bound lane before correcting its course to head north. They stated that they stayed a safe distance behind the driver because he was weaving in and out of his lane. Shortly after that they watched the car smash into the bicyclist killing her. I went back to the Clarion winery to inquire about guests who had recently departed the winery. The bartender mentioned that an elderly couple, four men with British accents and a loud, boisterous man had settled their checks and left the bar within the previous one half hour. In describing the single man he mentioned that he had served him two rounds of wine and then cut him off because he thought he was drunk. He also said that the man had had procured a third round from another customer who he had probably bribed to obtain more wine."

"Objection your honor. This is all hearsay and irrelevant," the defendant's attorney cried out. "Objection overruled," the judge replied. "This may have relevance to the case. Get on with it Officer O'Reilly," the judge said brusquely. "It is very relevant your honor. I had copies of the receipts from the last three groups of customers printed out. Then I had all the car rental agencies in the surrounding areas surveyed for a white sedan rental car registered to the names listed on the receipts. We found a match belonging to one of the customers, a Mr. Richard Kramer," he said. "And what did you learn?" the prosecutor asked. "We determined that Mr. Kramer had rented the sedan on Sept. 10, 2010 from the Didactic Car Rental Agency at the San Francisco airport. We obtained the license plate number and traced it to the Santa Rosa auto repair shop," he said. "Do you see Mr. Kramer in the courtroom?" he asked. "Yes sir. He is sitting with his defense lawyer right over there." All the eyes of the jury members turned to view Mr. Kramer. Jason read anger in the eyes of several of them. His hopes for a conviction were raised.

"I have no further questions your honor." Turning to the defense attorney the judge said. "It is your witness."

Mr. Sol Rosencrantz was a well respected criminal defense attorney from Los Angeles. He knew his client was in serious jeopardy. There was little room to muster up a reprieve and he knew it. "Officer O'Reilly are you sure the testimonies of Mr. Jason Gianelli and Mrs. Shea are valid?" he asked. "What do you mean?" O'Reilly answered. "They implied that my client had been drinking and was drunk. That's just speculation on their part. For all we know they were the ones drunk. Their vision may have been cloudy and distorted. Perhaps they only imagined they had witnessed an accident. Isn't that possible?" he said glowering at Officer O'Reilly. "Yes sir. That is possible." Mr. Rosencrantz smiled. "In that case they could have been mistaken. Isn't that a possibility?" he asked with a smug look on his face. "Yes, sir. In fact that same thought crossed my mind. I asked them if they had been visiting a winery just before the accident occurred," he said. "And what did they say?" he asked rather triumphantly. "They said they had been tasting wine at the Crouching Lion Winery just before they got into their car to head north on the Silverado Trail." "You see, Officer O'Reilly, they admitted to drinking at the Crouching Lion." "Yes sir, and for that reason I gave them both a Breath Analyzer test for alcohol to see if they were inebriated." "And what did it show?" Rosencrantz asked expectantly. "It didn't even register an alcohol level. I was surprised just as you are now!" There were some giggles from the back of the court room. "They both admitted to tasting the wine at the Crouching Lion but then spitting it out before swallowing any of it." Rosencrantz was visibly shaken and disappointed. He had not expected that answer. Turning to the judge he said. "I have no further questions your honor," and he sat down.

Jason felt a surge of jubilation and joy. He wanted to give O'Reilly a high five, but restrained himself. His advice to Stephanie about only tasting the wine had been wise. And Officer O'Reilly was to be congratulated for testing them with the Breath Analyzer. After Jason and Stephanie had given their testimonies and had been interrogated rather unsuccessfully by Rosencrantz, Brady Nelson was called to the stand. He had sandy hair and tear stained blue eyes. His anguish was palpable. He looked pitifully sad and the jury must have felt his pain.

After identifying himself, Roger Kirkpatrick, the plaintiff's attorney asked for his occupation. "I am a computer scientist with an internet related services company in Mountain View California," he said. "Where did you study computer science?" he asked. "I studied at Cal Tech where I received my PhD in computer science two years ago." "And then you joined this company?" he asked. "Yes sir." "What are you doing at this company?" he asked. "I am helping to develop a new sophisticated program for cloud computing," he replied. "How is it going?" "Well, I have just been granted two new patents that are showing promise in expanding and improving our program," he said. Jason could see that the jurors were impressed. He certainly was. "And what was your deceased wife's educational background?" "She received her PhD doctoral degree from the University of California Berkeley three years ago. She was two years younger than me and was one of the youngest graduate students to be awarded a PhD in the history of the University. She was the true brain in our family," he said modestly. "Where was she employed?" "She worked for a computer company in Cupertino California," he replied. "Had she received any patents?" "No, but her PhD thesis regarding computer mobile operating systems is being applied to modify and improve the current company's I OS system. They had very high hopes for her," and with that he broke down and cried. "We were looking so forward to raising our son together. Both of our companies allow their scientists to work independently with very flexible hours. We would have been able to spend lots of time with Brad, Jr. Now he is also gone," he lamented.

The women in the jury box were wiping tears from their eyes. They were moved by his testimony and the loss of his brilliant wife and unborn son. How could a drunken monster kill someone in broad daylight and then leave the scene of the accident without rendering aid of any kind. They glared at Kramer whose face showed no signs of remorse. Next Brady Nelson described the accident scene and reviewed how careful they had been to stay far to the right in their bike lane. His face showed signs of anger and despair as he left the stand. Rosencrantz did not have the courage to cross examine him. He knew the case had been settled. The evidence against his client was too overwhelming. He would not look forward to the cross examination of his client, Mr. Kramer.

Mr. Kramer took the oath and looked straight ahead with a stony face. He had a stocky build and a ruddy face. His eyes were ice cold and penetrating. There was no remorse in his demeanor.

Roger Kirkpatrick, the prosecuting attorney, asked for his name. "Richard Kramer," he said. "And what is your occupation Mr. Kramer?" "I am a defense attorney." "Do you specialize in defending criminals?" "I defend people who have allegedly committed crimes. They are innocent until proven guilty," Kramer said. "Does that mean the criminal must be found guilty in performing his or her criminal act?" "The defendant must be found guilty beyond any reasonable doubt to be convicted?" "Mr. Kramer we are charging you with vehicular manslaughter in the death of Melanie Brady and her unborn son. As a defense attorney held in high regard by many criminals in this state, we will prove without a reasonable doubt that you are guilty," Kirkpatrick stated. "Were you driving the white sedan that struck and killed Melanie Brady and her unborn son on September 13, 2010 at approximately 12:30 pm?"

"Objection your honor," Rosencrantz shouted. "That calls for a conclusion and is also inflammatory." "Objection sustained. Please Mr. Kirkpatrick show us evidence to support your allegation," the judge said. "Yes sir. I will do just that," he replied. Turning to Mr. Kramer he asked. "Did you rent a white sedan from the Didactic Rental Car Agency on September 10, 2010 at the San Francisco Airport Terminal?" "Yes, I did," Kramer replied. "We present the rental agreement as exhibit number one your honor." He first showed it to the jury before handing it to the judge. "What did you do after you rented the car until the morning of September 13, 2010?" "I drove to San Francisco and spent two days there shopping and sightseeing." "When did you arrive in Napa Valley and where did you stay?" "I arrived in Napa in the late afternoon on September 12, 2010 and checked into the Silverado Resort and Spa," he replied. Jason and Stephanie both gasped. He had been at the same resort with them on that same evening. What a coincidence they thought. "And what did you do on September 13, 2010?" he asked. "I played 9 holes of golf early in the morning," he said. "Then what did you do?" Kirkpatrick asked. "I decided to visit some of the Napa Valley wineries that are so famous." "Did you go to the Clarion Napa Valley Winery that morning?" he asked. "Yes, I did." "Before you arrived at the Clarion Napa Valley Winery did you stop at any other wineries?" "Not that I can recall," Kramer said. "Did you stop at the Crouching Lion for a drink for example?" Kirkpatrick asked. "I may have stopped there to look at the crouching lion in the courtyard." "But you didn't go inside to sample any of their excellent wines?" "I don't recall but it sounds like you have been there," Kramer said jokingly and laughed. No one in the court room thought it was amusing. Jason was watching the faces of the jurors. He put himself in their place and judged Mr. Kramer's remark to be callous. Kramer had killed two innocent people. Did the jury feel what Jason felt? Looking at their solemn faces again, he thought they did. "So you don't remember if you tasted some wine at the Crouching Lion. Is that right?" Kirkpatrick asked. "That's right," he replied. "Your honor I want to place this receipt from the Crouching Lion that contains Kramer's signature and credit card number on it with you as exhibit number two." He showed it to the jury saying. "It is a bill covering three rounds of wine tastings." Rosencrantz looked worried. His client was committing perjury and he could do nothing about it. "Are there any other wineries you can't remember visiting before settling into the Clarion Napa Valley Winery to drink wine?" he asked. "Not that I can recall." "Perhaps the wine made you forgetful for I have one more of your credit card receipts from the morning of September 13, 2010. It shows you had purchased a bottle of Cabernet Sauvignon and two servings of wine at the Bishop Mountain Winery which is just down the road from the Silverado Resort and Spa. The bartender there said he was surprised to see you drink the entire bottle of Cabernet Sauvignon so early in the day."

Richard Kramer had recently served as the defense attorney for a notorious LA criminal known as Marvin the "Mole." Despite flimsy evidence his client, the "Mole," was convicted and sentenced to a prison term. The "Mole" and his friends thought Mr. Kramer had botched the case and they were very angry. Kramer became depressed over the conviction and decided to leave LA to drink away his troubles at the Napa Valley wineries. It was true. By 10:45 am on September 13, 2010 he had already consumed an entire bottle of Cabernet Sauvignon. He was well on his way to becoming drunk.

Mr. Kirkpatrick continued and said. "I contend that you stopped at the Bishop Mountain Winery first. Then you went to the Crouching Lion to drink and from there to the Clarion Napa Valley Winery to drink more wine. The Clarion bartender said you were loud and boisterous, laughing loudly at your own jokes. He refused to serve you a third round because he thought you were drunk. He also said you had another customer buy you a third round. This all occurred in a space of just over two and one half hours. It would indicate that you had consumed an entire bottle of Cabernet Sauvignon along with eight tastings of wine when you finally drove off from the Clarion Napa Valley Winery. Mr. Kramer I contend that you were drunk when you drove your car into Melanie Brady killing her and her unborn son," he shouted.

Mr. Kramer stood up and yelled. "You have no proof of that. There are no blood tests or Breath Analyzer tests to support your allegations." Mr. Kirkpatrick responded in a steely voice and turning to the jury said. "What I have shown you is presumptive evidence supporting the fact that Mr. Kramer had consumed an entire bottle of wine and eight wine tastings between 10 am and 12:30 pm on September 13, 2010. That would be enough to make anyone drunk in my opinion. No, we cannot prove you were drunk Mr. Kramer. We only have presumptive evidence to make that allegation. What we do have are two witnesses who saw you weaving up the Silverado Trail after leaving the Clarion Napa Valley Winery and then striking and killing Melanie Brady and her unborn son with your rental sedan. Why didn't you stop after you struck her Mr. Kramer?" he asked. "The accelerator was stuck and I couldn't stop," he blurted out. "You mean to tell me and the jury that suddenly after driving all the way through San Francisco and then to the Napa Valley that suddenly your accelerator stuck after you slammed into an innocent bicyclist? That's preposterous Mr. Kramer. Your honor this man has lied repeatedly on the stand. Please take that into account when you render a judgment."

"Objection your honor," Rosencrantz bellowed. "He is again drawing a conclusion and his remarks are inflammatory." "Objection sustained," replied the judge.

Jason had taken pictures of the accident scene and they were labeled. The date and times were recorded on the bottom of each picture. The one showing Brady cradling his wife's blood spattered head with tears streaming down his cheeks was the most poignant. Brady's right hand was over her lower abdomen where their son was a stillborn. They were also shown to the jurors and added as an exhibit. The final exhibit consisted of pictures of the damaged sedan's right fender taken by the Santa Rosa auto repair shop.

Hate and anger filled the courtroom as the jurors retired to deliberate their verdict. One hour later they emerged. "Has the jury reached a verdict?" the judge asked? "We have your honor." "How do you find the defendant?" "We find him guilty your honor and request that you sentence him with the harshest penalties you can render."

# Chapter 35

AT HER NEXT appointment with Dr. Chang Valerie described her disappointment in not being able to control her recent harsh reaction to seeing Barry Greenberg at Jason Gianelli's option seminar. She described her efforts to quell her anger using Qigong and Kundalini Yoga stress reduction techniques. "They were not very effective," Valerie said. "I don't expect you to master these techniques in a few weeks or even months," Dr. Chang replied. "Your hatred toward Mr. Gianelli will continue to overwhelm you at times. Your reactions are just so intense and pervasive that you can't control your natural responses. With more time you'll improve your ability to reduce your anger and hostility." "How long will it take Dr. Chang?" Valerie asked. "I've never had anyone express as much latent and overt hostility toward another individual in all the years I have been involved with this program. Your reaction to Jason Gianelli is the most virulent I've ever encountered. Even patients who have significantly less hostility have sometimes taken up to a year before they can significantly reduce their stress reactions through meditation, prayer and relaxation techniques." "A year!" Valerie exclaimed. "Yes a year. In your case it could take two or more years," Dr. Chang replied. Valerie was shaken. Her eyebrows arched up in disbelief. "I am a very resolute person. I will conquer my reactions to Jason in under a year," she said. "You might be able to do that, but don't get discouraged if you're unsuccessful. Twenty four years of hostility have been embedded into your psyche. That's a long time and from what you have told me it has recently intensified," she said. "Yes it has. When Jason

took away one half of Dr. Friedman's account from me I was furious. I
hadn't realized that my reaction could produce a serious abnormal heart
rhythm. I just can't let that happen again. The possibility of a stroke fright-
ens me," she replied. "Then continue with your training classes Valerie.
These techniques will help you in many ways."

"I want you to know that Dr. Creighton, my orthopedic surgeon has
given me permission to join the La Jolla Life Improvement Center and I've
joined. I now have a certified personal trainer who is helping me meet my
fitness goals. Of course there are limitations due to my total knee replacement. I've already noticed some improvement in my muscle conditioning,
flexibility and strength," Valerie said. Dr. Chang was both pleased and encouraged by Valerie's efforts. She knew that supervised physical exertion
would help alleviate some of the stress in her life. Valerie continued by
saying. "I realize that I will have to wait before I can engage in a program to
improve my cardiovascular endurance. I also know that eventually this total
physical rehabilitation program will pay off when I'm able to resume playing
tennis. I've started the free-motion kinesis training program too. It will be a
few weeks before I can engage in using all the various cables, grips and
weight stacks." Dr. Chang noticed Valerie's enthusiasm as she described her
involvement in her dynamic training program and she was encouraged. If
Valerie could focus more on improving her physique, some of the emotional turmoil in her life would also be dissipated she thought. It was important to use all the facets of the Integrative Medicine program to produce
a life changing transformation. "Valerie I am so pleased with your progress.
With time I think you can achieve your goals."

Dr. Chang led Valerie out of her office and walked her out to the labyrinth. The labyrinth consisted of a series of carefully aligned rocks. They
were placed in concentric circles to form a path to and from the center
space. It was located in the center of a wide expanse of flat, well groomed
land just to the west of the La Jolla Center for Integrative Medicine. An
elliptical track surrounded the Labyrinth. A few joggers were running on the
track. Valerie looked longingly past the outdoor track to gaze out at the vast
Pacific Ocean. It was a serene and peaceful sight. The day would come
when she could jog again and eventually play tennis. That thought lifted her
spirits.

Dr. Chang explained that the design of the labyrinth was based upon sacred geometry. Its purpose was to help promote relaxation, spiritual growth and improved clarity of mind. "Valerie please close your eyes and take in slow deep breaths before we enter the Labyrinth," Dr. Chang said. Valerie was searching for a path toward inner peace. Could this walk bring her closer to that goal? As she slowly began to take in deep breathes, she inwardly hoped for some form of transformation.

"Now open your eyes and enter the labyrinth with me," Dr. Chang said. "As we move toward the center, let go of the stress in your life. This is the releasing phase of the walk." As Valerie slowly walked toward the center of the labyrinth, she began to relax. Why was she so tense? She was making progress toward controlling her anger and hostility toward Jason. Meditation and prayer were helping to reduce her anxiety. As the soothing ocean breeze caressed her face, she began to smile. The sun was warm. As she looked out over the Pacific Ocean, she began to expand her vision. She even began to experience feelings of joy and contentment. Her battles with Jason were losing their force and importance. Except for him her life was happy and fulfilling. Dr. Chang interrupted her thoughts. "Now as we enter the center of the labyrinth I want you to focus on receiving peace and tranquility," Valerie was experiencing a degree of serenity. She was grateful to be alive. Her health was being restored and she was becoming stronger and more resilient. Her transformation into a more loving and accepting person was taking place. There were glimmerings of hope.

"As we go back out to return to the outside world I want you to focus on any insights you may have received during this journey," Dr. Chang remarked. "I have gained some important insights during this walk," Valerie said. "I'm beginning to realize that my future will provide me with more satisfaction and fulfillment."

As they left the labyrinth, Valerie turned to Dr. Chang and said. "Thank you for introducing me to the labyrinth. It has helped me gain a broader perspective. As I walked through the labyrinth, I began to realize that my problems aren't very significant." "Whenever I walk the labyrinth I realize my rather insignificant place in the vast universe," Dr. Chang said. "My troubles are small compared to those so many other people are experiencing throughout the world. I end up giving thanks for all the opportunities I have been granted and for the friendships I have cultivated. As I walk in the labyrinth, my troubles tend to disappear."

"I gained some meaningful insights into what's important in my life too Dr. Chang." "I will bring my husband, Charles to the labyrinth. I would like to walk through it with him. I think it will help to strengthen our love for one another and broaden our horizons." "Can you imagine Jason Gianelli walking through the labyrinth with you Valerie?" Dr. Chang replied. "No, I can't!" Valerie exclaimed. She was shocked. Just the mention of Jason's name stirred up such bad feelings. "We will never go that far in our relationship," she said with emphasis. Dr. Chang was surprised by the intensity of Valerie's response. She thought the labyrinth would have softened such a violent reaction. Valerie was also dismayed. Her virulent reaction toward Jason persisted despite the more subdued feelings she had felt in the labyrinth. "I doubt that I will ever be able to walk the labyrinth with Jason," she said. "I can't even imagine it as a possibility."

Dr. Chang smiled. She hoped that perhaps in the future a miracle might occur. Yes, she thought. It might take a miracle to resolve Valerie's hatred toward Mr. Gianelli. "I'm going to leave you here to ponder that possibility Valerie. Please arrange to see me in an office follow up visit in four weeks," she said and she left.

As Valerie looked out upon the ocean and down toward the shoreline of La Jolla she began to wonder. What would it take to fully conquer her unhealthy reactions toward Jason? Would it take a miracle? Of course not. What a foolish notion. It would require the acquisition of better relaxation techniques. She didn't believe in miracles.

# Chapter 36

JASON AND STEPHANIE were jubilant over the guilty verdict as they left the court house to drive back down to La Jolla. The sentencing would occur in three more days and they would return to hear it. Jason took a swig of an antacid and two acetaminophen tablets to calm down his stomach. The excitement was churning his stomach he thought. He was happy over the guilty verdict. Now he was eager to resume his option trading.

The sentencing of Kramer was spectacular. The judge sentenced Mr. Kramer to six years in prison for his grievous action in killing Melanie Brady and her unborn son. The judge noted that he had fled the scene of the accident without stopping to render aid. That was an egregious omission according to the judge who pronounced his decisions with disdain. The $10,000 fine he levied was not surprising. The potential for a huge restitution settlement loamed over Kramer's head. That could really hurt him financially and they hoped it would. He was a most despicable man. He needed to bleed just as Melanie had bled to death from all of the internal injuries she sustained in the crash.

When he returned to the office Jason was surprised when Valerie walked up to him and welcomed him back. He had noticed some changes in Valerie's demeanor. She seemed more relaxed. He was amazed when she showed up for his options seminar. Was she actually going to do more than just sell covered calls and puts? "Valerie I am pleased that you are interested in my option strategies," he remarked. "I would like to see you involve yourself in some more sophisticated option trading techniques. They will potentially make you much more money than the ones you're currently employing." "Jason you are the pro when it comes to option action. It's still too daunting and risky for me," she replied. She seemed more cheerful and content. Jason was surprised and somewhat puzzled over the change.

That night Jason asked Stephanie if Valerie was taking a tranquilizer or some kind of happy pill. "No Jason she's not on a tranquilizer. Valerie is attending the La Jolla California Center for Integrative Medicine and it's producing some rather dramatic changes in her life. Her swimming routine mixed with something she calls the kinesis exercises are making her more fit. Besides that she is practicing yoga, deep breathing exercises and deep meditation. I may join the center too. Then we could go to classes together. I might become even more spiritual Jason," she remarked. "Wouldn't you like that?" He laughed. "It sounds like a sham to me Stephanie," he replied. "Well the positive results I'm seeing in Valerie are striking. She's much more content and serene," she said. "Do you think it will help mend the bad feelings she has toward me?" he asked. "That's hard to predict. You two have been fighting for years. About three months ago she started to cry over something you had done to her. She wouldn't tell me what it was over, but she seemed heartbroken. What did you do to her Jason?" she asked. He knew it had to do with the Dr. Friedman defection which he had so deceptively carried out. He couldn't tell Stephanie that he had actually stolen Valerie's computer files containing all of her client information. That was such an egregious act that even he felt a pang of guilt. Then he noticed more stomach distress and took more antacids and acetaminophen. He was sure he was developing an ulcer over the stress he was inflicting on other people as well as himself. He even recalled how he had stolen John Davenport's clients which had led to his eventual suicide. He knew that he was largely responsible for Davenport's death. "I just don't know what I could have done to cause her that much grief Stephanie," he lied. "I do know this Jason. Dr. Friedman has ascribed her stress as largely due to you. After the office party, she saw Dr. Friedman the following Monday. She developed some kind of heart rhythm disturbance that required treatment with an intravenous medicine. The doctor had warned her that it could potentially cause a stroke. Did you know about that?" she asked. "No, I had no idea she developed a heart rhythm problem," he remarked lying again.

He lied so effortlessly. Of course he had years of practice. For Jason lying was like drinking a glass of water. It was that easy. "If you're causing her this much distress, I hope you will stop it. If not for her, do it for me. She's my closest friend. I don't want to lose her to another heart attack or stroke." "She seems relaxed now," Jason said. "Well if stress can potentially kill her and you're responsible for the stress, please stop provoking her. In a way it would be just as bad as Mr. Kramer killing Melanie Brady. In your case you aren't drunk. You're in full possession of all your faculties. Why not change your behavior and try to make friends with her? Will you try?" she asked. "Sure I'll try," he said.

He wasn't sincere. Instead his response was superficial. Stephanie was so naive. He relished doing combat with Valerie. It brought out the worse side of him, but that's what competition was all about. It stimulated him to excel. That's why he had the most clients and the largest monthly paycheck in the firm. He wasn't ethical, but he could live with his conscience. Even if he caused Valerie's death, he would be sorry, but not for long. He would then take over most of her clients. That thought made him smile. In many ways he was as ruthless and unfeeling as Richard Kramer.

Jason threw himself back into option trading. Thanksgiving was approaching and, after a slow start, he was having an exceptional year in the 2010 market. The verdict on his call option strategy had come in on October 15, 2010. Each batch of 5 all options for his clients had given them a $33,000 profit. He had personally garnered $660,000 in profits. He financed a two month fully paid vacation for his mother to visit her relatives in Italy. He planned a wine tour of France with Stephanie during the summer of 2011. The spectacular returns generated by his call option strategy had more than erased the losses he had experienced in the first half of 2010. He decided to currently celebrate by taking a seven day skiing trip to the slopes surrounding Lake Tahoe in December. Over a Thanksgiving dinner at the La Jolla Tennis Club, Jason remarked to Stephanie. "I have rented a beautiful ski chalet close to the various Lake Tahoe ski resorts in northern California starting on December 8, 2010. The Lake Tahoe region is beautiful in the winter. Will you please join me for a skiing adventure?" "I would be delighted, but what if the snow is bad?" "Then we'll have to savor some outstanding Cabernet Sauvignons from Napa Valley around the hot tub.

There are some indoor activities we could enjoy too," he said. A mischievous grin appeared on his face. If the activities were anything like the ones they shared in Napa Valley, she would relish going she thought. As he ate, Jason noticed a gnawing discomfort in his stomach that went straight through to his back. It didn't stop even after he took two acetaminophen tablets and three swigs of an antacid. Stephanie noticed his discomfort too and said. "Jason, before we go skiing I want you to check out your ulcer symptoms. They seem to be worsening. I've even noticed that you've lost some weight. It could be something more serious," she said. "I just think I've been worrying too much. Some of my option trades could deteriorate before the year ends and that has me concerned. I've had a phenomenal year so far. I don't want to lose any of my gains in the last month of the year. To satisfy you I'll call my internist on Monday and try to schedule an appointment before we go on the ski trip."

Jason's internist, Dr. Charles Chandler, had taken 10 days off and wouldn't be back in time to see Jason before his scheduled ski trip. Jason made an appointment for December 16, 2010 just nine days before Christmas.

The snow at the Lake Tahoe ski resorts was fine and they were enjoying themselves. Stephanie noticed that Jason's skiing routine had radically changed. He wasn't racing down the black runs and was quiting after only three hours of skiing. Normally he would ski all day and sometimes even at night under the lights.

Drinking wine around the hot tub was wonderful. Stephanie noticed some of Jason's muscles had shrunk and she asked. "Have you been decreasing your gym workouts Jason?" "Yes I have," he replied. "Why do you ask?" "Well it seems to me you have lost some muscle mass and your vitality has diminished. You're also only skiing three hours a day instead of your usual six hours. What's made you change?" "My stamina has decreased over the past few months. I'm not sure why. I thought maybe it's my ulcer," he said. "Does an ulcer do that?" she asked. "I'm not sure but we'll soon find out. I have an appointment with my internist next week, the day after we return from this ski trip."

They ate at some fabulous restaurants located around Lake Tahoe. Stephanie enjoyed the meals but she noticed Jason often left food on his plate. No wonder he was losing weight. She was sure that he had dropped at least 10 pounds. "Jason, you need to eat more, You have always relished deserts and now you are not even ordering them." "I just don't have much of an appetite. When I eat my stomach discomfort seems to worsen," he said. Stephanie was alarmed. She thought ulcer symptoms were usually alleviated by eating. Perhaps that wasn't true for hot spicy foods, but that wasn't what they were ordering. She had a foreboding feeling. Jason might be suffering from something other than an ulcer. Could it be cancer? The very thought terrified her. She had lost her first husband to cancer and could not bear to lose Jason in the same way.

Their lovemaking had suffered too. Jason seemed less interested in making love with Stephanie during this ski trip. It was a radical departure from the intense expressions of love they had experienced in Napa Valley. She attributed it in part to vacationing in Tahoe. It was true that the surrounding mountains were beautiful. Looking down on Lake Tahoe from some of the high mountain slopes was breathtaking. But it was cold. It wasn't the warm sunshine they had so enjoyed in the Napa Valley. She recalled how much they had appreciated the variety of scenery and pleasures during their Napa Valley trip. This trip was in so many ways a letdown. After the fourth day, she looked forward to their return to La Jolla. Jason wasn't enjoying the trip very much either. He had lost his zest for skiing. That surprised him. Other than golf skiing had become his favorite sport. He had been so pleased by his golfing results at the Silverado Resort and Spa last September. Maybe they should return to the Napa Valley. He had noticed in the past few weeks while playing golf in La Jolla that his drives were becoming shorter. He was starting to miss greens on his second shot on par four holes. His handicap had gone up five strokes in just the past two months. He was deteriorating and that alarmed him.

# Chapter 37

JASON WAS TAKEN into one of Dr. Chandler's examining rooms at the La Jolla Clinic. He began to ponder his health status. Valerie's right knee had been replaced. Her heart attack had been averted by the nimble and skilled hands of Dr. Friedman. Now it was his turn to be diagnosed and treated. His last complete physical exam and testing had been performed in early January of 2009 almost two years ago. Everything had been normal at that time. In fact he had nearly gone the distance on the treadmill stress test and there were no EKG abnormalities detected. His blood tests had been normal including his lipid panel. Stephanie insisted on a colonoscopy for Jason since her former husband had died of metastatic colon cancer. Her husband had cancelled his scheduled colon exams twice to attend business meetings and failed to ever reschedule them. He died four years later of metastatic colon cancer. Stephanie didn't want the same fate for Jason. She was relieved when his colonoscopy was reported to be normal.

He knew that there was something drastically wrong with him now. He realized that he had not scheduled his annual doctor's examination in 2010. He was nearly one year late. I deserve to have some health issues considering all the hateful things I have done to Valerie, John Davenport and others in the firm he thought.

Dr. Chandler listened carefully to Jason's account of his abdominal distress. "When was the first time you noted any kind of stomach discomfort," he asked. In thinking back Jason realized that he had first noted some discomfort in early April 2010 over nine months ago. It had been barely noticeable then, but he cited it. "Over the last three months it has become more frequent and worse Dr. Chandler. I thought it was an ulcer and started taking an antacid for relief," he said. "Did it help?" Dr. Chandler asked. "I thought so at first, but then I noticed that I had to also take 500 milligrams of acetaminophen to relieve the pain. At first one was enough. Now I have to take two every 3 to 4 hours to control the pain." Jason said. Dr. Chandler's face registered alarm. "Don't you drink alcohol?" he asked. "Of course I do. I usually have one or two glasses of wine with dinner every night. Sometimes, if it is a special vintage, I will even have a third glass. Why do you ask?" "I prefer to limit the dose of acetaminophen allowed in 24 hours to 4000 milligrams which is eight 500 mg tablets a day," Dr. Chandler replied. "Beyond that liver damage may occur, but it's rare. It can be aggravated by the intake of alcohol. I will definitely order a liver battery on you to see if any damage has occurred from the combination of acetaminophen and alcohol. Have you lost any weight?" he asked. "Yes I think I've lost a few pounds. I haven't weighed myself in months, so I can't give you a figure." Jason said. "Show me where the pain is located," Dr. Chandler said. "It's right in the middle of my stomach," Jason said. He placed his hand directly above his belly button. "Does it radiate anywhere from there?" Dr. Chandler asked. "It seems to go right through to my back. Lately I've also experienced some pain in the upper right side of my abdomen," Jason said. After questioning him in depth, Dr. Chandler proceeded to examine him. When he finished he said. "There are three things that alarm me. You have lost twenty five pounds since I weighed you last in January 2009. I feel something firm in your mid abdomen. Your liver is also enlarged." "What do those findings mean?" Jason asked. "I'm not sure, but I will order some tests that will clarify these findings," Dr. Chandler replied.

"You have worried over a possible ulcer. The symptoms you've described are different than those commonly associated with an ulcer. I will schedule an appointment with a gastroenterologist to investigate that possibility. He can also evaluate your enlarged liver. As to the abdominal findings, I'll order a Computerized Tomography study of your abdomen." "Is that a CT scan?" Jason asked. "Yes, it is. In addition I will have blood drawn for liver studies, a lipid panel, blood count, and several other studies. Within the next two weeks we should have some definitive answers. Do you have any questions?" Dr. Chandler asked. "I want you to do everything necessary to make a precise diagnosis doctor. I have promised my girlfriend that I'm willing to have a complete and thorough investigation of my condition." he said. Jason was afraid to ask the question that was plaguing him. He wanted to ask. Could this be cancer? He just couldn't get the words out of his mouth. He knew a diagnosis of cancer would devastate Stephanie and it would be agonizing for him too. In this way he could honestly say that Dr. Chandler had not definitively addressed the question of cancer. Even in this he was devious he thought. "No I don't have any questions," he replied. "Then please take this order sheet out to the scheduler and let's get started on your evaluation."

The fasting blood studies had been done the day after his examination. The abdominal CT study was performed on the following day. It would be two weeks before a gastroenterologist could see him. After all, Christmas was just around the corner. Doctors took Christmas vacations too.

He was surprised when his secretary buzzed him with an urgent call from Dr. Chandler in the afternoon following his morning abdominal CT scan. "Tell him I will call him back as soon as I finish with my client," he said. She buzzed him back saying. "He won't hang up until you talk to him. He insists that you talk to him now." Jason was exasperated, but he excused himself and went out of his office to take the phone call from his secretary's desk. "What is it Dr. Chandler?" he asked. "I have just reviewed the results of your abdominal CT scan with the radiologist Jason. It's very important that you come to my office today. Please come to my office at four pm." Jason looked at his schedule. He would have to cancel his last two appointments. "Can we possibly change that to four pm tomorrow?" he asked. "No Jason. This can't wait," he said. "O.K.," Jason said. "I'll see you at four pm today." "Thank you," Dr. Chandler replied. "I will be waiting for you in my office."

Jason was alarmed. This had to be serious. He was taken back to Dr. Chandler's office by a nurse. Dr. Chandler greeted Jason and said. "Come over to my x-ray viewing boxes and take a look at your abdominal CT pictures. I am afraid I have bad news for you. Do you see this mass?" he said pointing to a large lump. "Yes," replied Jason. "It measures 4 by 6 inches Jason and it's located in your pancreas." Jason feared the worse. He had difficulty asking the question. "Could it be cancer?" Jason whispered. "Yes, I'm afraid that it's cancer," he replied. "If it is removed, can I be cured?" Jason asked hopefully. "I'm sorry Jason but that's not the whole story. This is your liver," he said pointing to another structure. "It contains six worrisome spots." "What does that mean?" Jason inquired. "I think these spots represent metastases from your pancreatic tumor." "It has already spread to my liver?" Jason asked in disbelief. "Yes, I think that's the case." "What do we do next Dr. Chandler?" Jason asked. "I will arrange for two needle biopsies. One will enter the pancreatic mass. The other will enter one of the liver spots. Once we have a tissue diagnosis we can outline a treatment program for you," he said.

Jason was stunned. Stephanie had been right. He should have had a doctor's appointment months ago. In retrospect this process had been going on for at least several months. Perhaps it was present more than a year ago. He had read that pancreatic cancer was usually silent until it had significantly grown and even spread. He wondered if the diagnosis could have been made in April 2010 when he first noticed a tinge of abdominal discomfort. He had ignored it. Option trading dominated his thinking and precluded any thought of health issues.

"I will do whatever you advise Dr. Chandler," he said weakly. Dr Chandler filled out some scheduling forms and directed him to the lobby schedulers. He also handed him a prescription for Vicodin. "Vicodin will be more effective in controlling your abdominal pain than acetaminophen Jason. We have stronger analgesics in case Vicodin doesn't work."

Jason's life was suddenly imploding. He had read about several famous people who had battles with pancreatic cancer. They had not been pleasant. But he also knew one of the high tech giants had been diagnosed with pancreatic cancer several years ago and he was still alive. He had undergone an operation to remove his pancreatic tumor and later he had a liver transplant in 2009. It was now the end of 2010 and he was still alive. Jason felt a surge of hope. He would gladly submit to pancreatic and liver surgery if they would save his life. I'm too young to die he thought. I will conquer this.

Suddenly option trading had lost its significance. He would have to eventually tell Stephanie. He decided to delay telling her until after the biopsies had been performed and a definitive diagnosis had been rendered. He needed to know what his options consisted of should metastatic pancreatic cancer be proven. He hadn't told Stephanie about his trip to Dr. Chandler's office today. His discussion with her would have to wait.

Ten days later the biopsy reports had been issued. Jason's case had been carefully reviewed during the weekly La Jolla Clinic tumor board meeting. Specialists in oncology, radiation therapy, surgery, radiology, pathology and several other disciplines had convened to evaluate his findings and make recommendations for treatment. In Jason's case chemotherapy and radiation therapy had been advised. Jason's oncologist informed him of the findings and recommendations. "Mr. Gianelli you have a pancreatic adenocarcinoma. It has spread from your pancreas to involve abdominal lymph nodes and both lobes of the liver. We can only offer you palliative treatment." "Which means I'm going to die?" Jason asked. The oncologist only nodded yes. "I'm sorry Mr. Gianelli. The cancer is too far advanced to be surgically curable." Jason was shattered. He hadn't expected this. "Can I still see one of the liver transplant surgeons? I would like to hear it from him too." he said. "I can do that for you Mr. Gianelli. I will have the scheduler make you an appointment. When would you like to start chemotherapy and radiation treatments?" he asked. "Let me digest this for a week or two. I need to discuss it with some people," he said. "May I set up a follow up appointment with you in let's say 10 days?" the oncologist asked. "That will be fine," Jason said. "Just give this scheduling slip to my secretary for that appointment. I will go over the drugs we use to treat pancreatic cancer at that time," he said.

Jason finally had to reveal his diagnosis to Stephanie. She had been badgering him for information for the last two weeks. He had held her off with a series of lies. He claimed the Christmas holidays had delayed appointments. It seemed logical even if it wasn't true. He invited her to dinner at his home. He barbecued steaks out on his patio. The sunset was glorious with brilliant shades of red and subtle shades of purple and lavender. Stephanie began to sob as he told her his diagnosis. She couldn't stand to lose Jason to cancer. It was just too much for her to bear. She clung to him. "Why did this have to happen?" she wailed. "You're so young and vital." They ate their meal in silence broken by Stephanie's sobs. Jason was already depressed. He wanted to deny the diagnosis but the evidence was overwhelming. He mentioned a liver transplant to Stephanie holding it out as a ray of hope. She grasped at it. "Would you consent to a liver transplantation Jason?" she asked. "I would if there was a chance I could obtain a cure," he said. "They would also have to remove the tumor in the pancreas." He knew the tumor had spread too far for either operation to result in a cure, but he wanted to extend Stephanie some hope. "I'll look into all the options too, Jason. I'll comb the medical literature and search out the best surgeons in the country. I think we should consider a second opinion, perhaps at the Mayo Clinic or at Sloan Kettering," she said. "I understand that MD Anderson is also a top notch cancer center," Jason replied. "I'll go with you Jason. We have the resources to pay for the best treatment. What good is money if you can't spend it usefully," she added.

Jason and Stephanie had attended the appointment with the transplant surgeon at the La Jolla Clinic together. Stephanie had read that in some cases a partial liver transplantation from a living donor could be done. She was tested and met the requirements. She was willing to undergo the procedure if it would help Jason survive. "I'm terribly sorry Mr. Gianelli but your tumor cannot be removed for a cure. It has spread to both lobes of your liver and to abdominal lymph nodes. Even a living partial liver donation by Mrs. Shea would not result in a cure," he said. They were gravely disappointed. A liver transplantation would not be curative and he rejected their plea to do it anyway. They sought a second opinion from the Mayo Clinic transplantation team and they were given the same answer. The pancreatic tumor had spread too far to be surgically cured. Jason was left with palliative chemotherapy and radiation treatments. He finally started them in mid January 2011.

# Chapter 38

STEPHANIE HAD NO one to lean on except Valerie. She arranged a meeting with her at Valerie's home stating it was an emergency. It was an emotional emergency. Jason had asked her to keep his diagnosis a secret. She couldn't do that. She had to at least tell Valerie and seek her guidance and support.

Stephanie took Brady with her to Valerie's home. Valerie and Charles welcomed Stephanie into their home as Sasha darted to Brady's side. Charles took the two dogs outside to the backyard to play. Then he joined Valerie and Stephanie in the living room. "I just had to see you tonight," Stephanie said. She appeared crestfallen. There was despair in her eyes. "What's happened Stephanie? You look so sad," Valerie said. "It's Jason," she replied. "He has been diagnosed as having inoperable cancer." "What?" Valerie cried out. She stood up and rushed over to Stephanie. They clung to one another. Tears were streaming down from Stephanie's eyes. "We're so sorry Stephanie. We want to help you," Valerie said. "Are you sure it's inoperable?" Charles asked. "Yes, we even flew to the Mayo Clinic for a second opinion. They also said it was inoperable. He's only left with palliative chemotherapy and radiation treatments. He's going to slowly die. I went through this with my deceased husband and his metastatic colon cancer. It was a horrible experience."

Valerie and Charles searched their hearts for ways to comfort Stephanie. "We want to do everything we can to help you through this crisis Stephanie," Valerie said. "We know how much Jason means to you." "He means everything to me," Stephanie said. "Our trip to Napa Valley was the happiest time in my life. We looked forward to repeating it on my next birthday. I can't bear the thought of losing him." Her face was filled with grief and her shoulders slumped in despair.

Valerie's own acute illnesses had been conquered quickly. She could have died with her heart attack or been crippled by a stroke. Neither one had occurred. She was now well into a physical and emotional transformation through her participation in the programs sponsored by the La Jolla Center for Integrative Medicine. Her muscle tone had improved. Most of all her emotions were under much better control. Even her hatred toward Jason was softening. Meditation, relaxation exercises and prayer were working wonders.

"Stephanie, I do have one suggestion for you. I would like you to join me and take part in the La Jolla Center for Integrative Medicine programs. I know deep meditation practices will help reduce your feelings of depression, anxiety, and loneliness. They are certainly helping me. We can attend the classes together. You already have prayer partners in your bible study group. They'll help lift your spirits. What do you think of that idea?" Valerie asked. Stephanie had previously thought of joining the Integrative Medicine programs before Jason was diagnosed with cancer. She could now participate in the programs with her best friend. A fleeting look of relief crossed her face. "I would like to do that with you Valerie." Above all she needed Valerie's companionship and support. She couldn't handle her emotions alone.

"What programs have helped you?" Stephanie asked. "Kundalini Yoga has helped me become more resilient," Valerie replied. "It has helped me accept and deal with the many challenges that have been thrust into my life. It's helping me in my search for more happiness and inner peace. Besides feelings of anger and hostility I have experienced periods of depression too. We can search for inner peace together Stephanie."

Jason's impending death was hard for Valerie to comprehend. He had always been so strong and full of energy. She couldn't imagine him dying at his young age of 50. They had been locked in battle for a long time. With his demise her conflicts with him would end. She knew gaining freedom from that ordeal would bring her tremendous relief. Yet she wanted Jason to live for Stephanie's sake. They were deeply in love and Jason made Stephanie happy. As much as she disliked Jason, she was not heartless. She wished he would survive to continue his love for Stephanie.

"Valerie do you think you could ever become Jason's friend?" Stephanie asked. "I have to be honest with you. Jason has been my enemy and rival for the past 24 years. He has caused me incredible levels of grief and even despair. I'm trying to change my attitude toward him but it's been a struggle," she replied. "But now Jason is dying. When he dies your battles with him will end. Please try to make amends with him before he dies. Do this for me. Please do it for me," she pleaded. Stephanie looked so sad and pitiful. Valerie was agonizing over her best friend's grief. "I will try to do it for you," Valerie replied. "Thank you," Stephanie said. "It would mean a lot to me. I think it would mean a lot to Jason too."

Valerie reviewed her longstanding feud with Jason. Her anger and hostility had been modified but they still existed. They had never settled their differences. Up to now they were still competing for clients. Although Valerie's ability to handle stress was improving, distrust and hostility toward Jason lingered. Now she, like Stephanie was in as state of turmoil.

Jason was the only person Valerie had ever hated in her entire life. She felt that her hatred was justified. Could she justify carrying that hate into Jason's grave? She struggled over the idea of forgiving him completely. In her heart she knew it would be the right thing to do. It would free her of the emotional burden hate carried with it. She decided to pray and to meditate over it.

Eventually Stephanie would need another man to love and console her. For the past three years Jason had been the only man in her life. She was deeply in love with him. To lose him would be for her a shattering experience. "Please help me through this ordeal, Valerie," Stephanie pleaded. "I know I can't do it alone." "I will stand by you, Stephanie," Valerie said. "You can count on me for support. I will try to resolve my anger and hatred toward Jason for your sake too." "Don't do it only for me Valerie. Do it for yourself. Your hostility toward Jason has already shortened your life. Your heart attack could have killed you and a stroke could have crippled you. I believe Jason played a major role in precipitating both of those health issues and you know it. Discard your hatred toward Jason while he is still alive. Why carry your hatred toward him all the way to his grave?"

# Chapter 39

JASON WAS ABOUT to start chemotherapy the next day. He invited Stephanie to an ocean front restaurant in La Jolla for dinner. With the start of chemotherapy and also staged radiation treatments he was sure his appetite would suffer. He wanted to share a delicious meal with her before that happened. He also wanted to enjoy what little time he had left to make her happy.

Deep inside him he knew what Stephanie wanted most in their relationship. He decided to offer it to her that night. The desert had been served. Jason had paid the corkage fee to have one of his favorite bottles of cabernet sauvignon served. It was a Vintage 2002 Staglin Family Vineyard Estate Cabernet Sauvignon. "This has one of the best bouquets and aromas of any wine I have ever savored," Jason said. Stephanie was practicing the wine drinking technique she had been taught by Jason in Napa Valley. Again she partially choked as she tried to pass inhaled air over the wine on her tongue and in the back of her throat. She laughed. "I just cannot master your wine drinking technique Jason. Please show me again how you do it." After swirling the wine for 30 seconds, Jason placed his head deeply into the glass and rested his forehead on the rim. Then he inhaled slowly through his nose. "For me this is the best part of enjoying Cabernet. It is the nose that I find exquisite. My olfactory nerve endings are stimulated by a fine wine and this one qualifies," he said. Stephanie was amused and smiled over his use of the word olfactory. "Do you mean your nose sniffing nerves become happy?" she asked with a grin. "Exactly," he replied. Then he took a sip of the wine and rolled it over his tongue. Taking in a slow shallow breathe, he smiled as the wine generated intense flavors. Stephanie looked at him lovingly. "You do that so well. No wonder you enjoy wines so much," she remarked. "You are the most important part of my wine tasting. Savoring a great glass of wine with you makes the experience very special," he replied.

He reached into his coat pocket and removed a small beautifully wrapped package. "I want us to always remember this night. Please accept this gift from me," he said. She carefully removed the gift paper. Then she read the message on the card that was attached to the box out loud, but softly so those in surrounding tables couldn't hear her. I bestow this gift to the one who has captured my heart. I love you Stephanie, signed Jason. She opened the box and gasped. It contained a five carat diamond engagement ring. Jason knelt down beside her and asked. "Will you marry me Stephanie?" Now heads turned. They had heard Jason's proposal and they smiled. Stephanie cried with joy. "I would love to marry you Jason." He slipped the ring onto her finger. The diamond sparkled. "Let us see it!" people cried out from nearby tables. Stephanie lifted her hand and proudly displayed the diamond ring to the onlookers. Several women exclaimed. "It's beautiful. Congratulations." One turned to Jason and said. "You're a very lucky man!" He beamed. "I know. She will make a wonderful bride and after that an incredible wife," he replied. People all around them were smiling. Stephanie thought their smiles and happiness would turn to frowns and sadness if they discovered Jason had pre-terminal cancer. You wouldn't know it though. Jason had a broad grin on his face and he seemed very happy. He gave Stephanie a hug and a warm kiss. Stephanie was ecstatic. She had wanted to be married to Jason for the last two years. It was finally happening. If only it could last. She buried her head in her handkerchief and started to cry. Jason quickly ordered the check and paid for it in cash. He left a hefty tip and they left.

When they reached the car Stephanie looked into Jason's eyes and said. "You don't have to marry me just because you are dying." "But I want to marry you. You are the most wonderful person I have ever met. I love you with all of my heart. We should have taken the opportunity to get married in the wedding chapel at the Silverado Resort and Spa. I wanted to marry you then and I still want to marry you now," he said. "I wanted to marry you in Napa too. We would have so enjoyed our honeymoon there," she replied. "Let's pretend that was our honeymoon. On the other hand we could fly back up there to actually have a short but wonderful honeymoon for a few days," he suggested. "I would love to do that!" she exclaimed. "Is there a special place you want to revisit up there?" he asked. "Yes there is a very special place. I would like to return to Jade Lake. I felt a deep peace and sense of tranquility there. I would like to share those feelings again with you," she replied. "We could toast each other over special glasses of wine. I recently bought two incredible bottles of Cabernet Sauvignon in a private auction," he said. "Let's do it Jason!" she exclaimed. "First let's get married'" he replied. "Let's get married next week and then return to Napa Valley," he said. They were both excited over the thought. He was about to say. I don't have much time left, but suppressed the words. The thought of becoming a widow again crossed Stephanie's mind and it alarmed her. She would lose her second husband to cancer. She vowed to make the time as Jason's wife memorable.

The small private wedding ceremony took place the following Sunday at the catholic church in La Jolla. Robert Kaplan served as Jason's best man and Valerie was Stephanie's bridesmaid. Only Charles Goldin and the priest were otherwise present. Valerie had advised Stephanie not to send out wedding invitations to any of Jason's co-workers. She knew they wouldn't attend.

There was no wedding reception. Stephanie had wanted some of her friends to attend their wedding and a reception afterwards. She especially wanted some of her friends from her bible class to attend. Then she thought they might be alarmed over Jason's deteriorating health. Perhaps they would question her decision to marry a dying man. She didn't care what they thought. She was happy. Soon they would be back in Napa Valley and that thought warmed her heart.

"It won't be long before we will revisit Jade Lake Jason. Do you remember the peace and love we experienced there?" she asked. "Yes, I do," he replied. "Before we go back could you let that same loving spirit fill your heart and start apologizing to everyone you have hurt?" she asked. Jason laughed. "That would take a long time. I've hurt a lot of people," he said.

"Why don't you start with the one you have hurt the most?" she asked. "You mean Valerie don't you?" he asked. "Yes I mean Valerie. She won't beg you for an apology. You know she deserves it so let loose and give it to her. Unburden yourself. An apology will help you bury your guilt." "Let me think about it," he replied. She was disappointed in him. Why couldn't he just open his heart and apologize to those he had wronged especially Valerie. She thought it would be so easy for him to apologize. Perhaps she didn't fully understand Jason's basic nature. She was oblivious to the fact that Jason was basically self centered and in so many ways insensitive. He had hidden those aspects of his character from her well.

# Chapter 40

JASON POSTPONED HIS chemotherapy and radiation treatments for four days. They were only going to spend three days in Napa Valley. Of course they returned to the Silverado Resort and Spa. Jason had trouble playing nine holes of golf. The same golf pro who had admired Jason's swing in September was alarmed when he watched Jason's weak drive off the first tee. Jason's appearance had drastically changed in only four months. That night Jason tried to make love with Stephanie, but it was an effort. The passion they had experienced last September had vanished. But Stephanie was still grateful for all the attention Jason bestowed upon her. "Thank you for marrying me Jason," she said. "I have wanted to be Mrs. Gianelli for a long time. I have dreamed for the day I could be called your wife. We must cherish every moment we have together."

They couldn't bear to drive north up the Silverado Trail. The vision of Brady and Melanie Nelson still haunted them. Instead they cut over to highway 29 and headed north. As they passed one of the famous wineries, Jason remembered that he had promised to take Stephanie on the twilight wine tour on her birthday the following year. He decided to return later in the day in order to take in that tour. There would not be any birthday celebration in 2011. The next day they drove up to Chateau Montelena and Jade Lake. Jason carried a special bottle of Cabernet Sauvignon along with a lunch basket out to the Pavilion on Jade Lake. Jason had to agree. It was a serene and peaceful place. Stephanie was praying silently to herself. "Please Lord accept Jason into your heavenly presence. Fill his heart with joy. Help him repent all of his sins." She felt a great calm pervade her mind and body. Perhaps it was the Holy Spirit she thought. If only Jason could become a Believer before he died. Perhaps it would happen. If he would only open his heart and repent for any wrong doings he may have committed during his lifetime. Was he too hardened in his ways? She could only hope and pray for his salvation.

"Let's have some lunch and enjoy our wine," Jason said breaking into her reverence. "I'd like that," she said. Her thoughts turned to Valerie. How would she handle Jason's gradual demise? Would Jason regret all the torment he had generated in her life? "The wine is incredible," she said. "It's one of my overall favorites," he replied. "That's why I brought it along. What better place exists in the whole world to enjoy it than on Jade Lake?" If he only knew the depth of reverence Jade Lake represented in her life, she thought. "I think the weeping willows agree with you. See how they are swaying in consent," she remarked. "You are the consummate romantic. Besides that you possess a vivid imagination. I haven't noticed the willows talking to me," he said. "I say what I feel and I feel a deep sense of serenity here. Can't you feel it too?" she asked. "I do feel something special here. I can't exactly describe it." Stephanie was pleased. "Just let the atmosphere of tranquility and reverence fill your soul. Let go of all your frustrations and bad feelings," Stephanie said. "Celebrate all of your accomplishments and good deeds."

"I wish I had worked with Valerie and not against her for all these years," Jason said. "She's such a good person. I just wouldn't allow myself to become her friend. I feel so guilty over all the torment I have caused her." "Perhaps she'll forgive you if you apologize to her," she said. "I could try," he replied. "But you must feel it in your heart Jason. It can't be superficial. It has to be sincere." Jason knew she was right. He had been duplicitous in most of his dealings with Valerie over the years. Their rivalry was something he relished. Now he was finally sorry for what he had done, but it took dying to realize that fact. "I don't think she'll accept my apology. She will construe it to be false," he said. "If you open up your heart to her and truly mean what you say, I think she will accept your apology. She is a warm and generous person. Her practice of deep meditation and prayer has led her to a different and better place," Stephanie said. "Try her out. Give her a chance to forgive you. I honestly think she would forgive you if you offered her the chance."

Jason recounted all the times he had frustrated Valerie over the years. His most egregious act was to steal her client account files from her office computer and persuade the Friedmans to turn over half of their account with Valerie to him. Yes, it was true. The Friedmans had recanted and removed Jason from their account. Valerie still didn't know that he had invaded her computer. That would be a secret that would die with him. He couldn't confess to that act. No one not even Stephanie would forgive him. Valerie had been right when she had called him a thief and a liar.

"I'm glad we decided to return to Napa together," he said. "This is where we have shared our most precious moments." "I agree. We'll enjoy the three days we have to spend here," she replied. She had envisioned a glorious return to Napa Valley on her next birthday. That dream had been shattered. Now she was left with a dying man and a dying dream. A profound sadness enveloped her. Her married life with Jason would soon end. It was going to be much too brief. When he died she would again experience a profound depression. This time it could be devastating. Valerie might gain a sense of freedom and liberation upon Jason's death. Stephanie's loss would be Valerie's gain. It made no sense to her. Why did they have to be enemies? She had to suppress her tears. She didn't want to destroy the harmony and love that existed between them right now. "Do you hear the birds singing?" she asked. "They are happy nesting in the trees around the lake. What freedom and joy they must have living in a beautiful sanctuary like this. They must love this place just as I do," she said. "I will always cherish the time we have shared here," he said. "Of course savoring this great bottle of wine has helped too." "Yes, but I am convicted by a deeper sense of love and harmony here," she replied. Stephanie would have to let him go soon. Wrapping her arms around him tightly she gave him a loving kiss. His lips were somewhat cold. She didn't like that. It portended death.

After another hour had elapsed Jason said. "Let's go back to the Culinary Institute for dinner." "I wish we had recognized the significance of your stomach distress when we last ate there. It signaled something was wrong," Stephanie said. "Do you think it would have made a difference if your pancreatic cancer had been diagnosed then?" "I don't think so. It was most likely already too late. We'll never know," Jason replied. He was probably right. Since his diagnosis had been rendered, Stephanie had studied pancreatic cancer in depth. When it caused pain or discomfort it had already invaded the pancreatic capsule and most likely spread through the blood stream to the liver and other places. It was one of the stealthiest cancers in existence. She wondered. Why did it have to happen to Jason?

The waiter remembered them at the restaurant. Jason's tip had been the largest he had ever received. The waiter was dismayed when he noticed how much weight Jason had lost just since their last visit. "What would you like to drink?" the sommelier asked Stephanie. She deferred to Jason. "She would like to try a glass of the 1999 Spottswoode Estate Vineyard Cabernet Sauvignon," Jason said. The sommelier was pleased. "That's one of our finest vintages," he said. "What may I serve you sir?" "I will have a glass of your 1991 Robert Mondavi Reserve Cabernet Sauvignon," Jason said. "You have also selected one of our best wines," he said with admiration. "Just out of curiosity do you have a bottle of the 1995 Screaming Eagle Cabernet Sauvignon in your cellar?" Jason asked. "Yes we do. We have three bottles left. Would you like to try a glass?" he asked. "I will defer for now. Thank you for asking," Jason replied. Stephanie interjected. "I don't see Screaming Eagle listed in your wine book." "It's a very distinct blend madam. Most people would wince at the price and not order it. Your husband obviously knows wines. It's a superb blend of 88% Cabernet Sauvignon, 10% Merlot, and 2% Cabernet Franc. One of the foremost wine critics gave it 99 points!" he exclaimed. "Just how expensive is one glass?" she asked. "We are selling it for $750 a glass," he replied. Stephanie gasped. "$750 for just one glass?" she said in disbelief. "Yes that's the price for a single glass. Only wine connoisseurs order it," he said. "They have to be rich too," she added. "When was the last time you served a glass?" "It was approximately three months ago. A gentleman and his wife from Paris ordered a bottle. They said that they wanted to compare the Screaming Eagle to some of France's finest Bordeaux vintages," he said. "Did they like it?" she asked. "Yes they did. They admitted to me that it rivaled the finest wines they had ever tasted. I loved the way they said it too with their rich French accents. It made me proud to be a sommelier in Napa Valley."

Jason had virtually no appetite and only ordered a piece of prime New York steak cooked medium rare. It would complement his wine. Stephanie didn't know much about wine pairings and ordered a Caesar salad followed by Halibut. Jason smiled. "I should have ordered you a Chardonnay to go with the Halibut instead of a Cabernet," he remarked. "I like the Spottswoode Jason. I think it would go well with anything. It's heavenly," she said.

Before leaving Napa Valley the next day Jason called the Napa Valley police station. "Is Officer O'Reilly in?" he asked. "Yes he is. May I tell him who is calling?" "Please tell him it's Jason Gianelli." "Mr. Gianelli what a pleasant surprise," O'Reilly said. "What brings you to town?" "We're celebrating our honeymoon," he replied. "That's wonderful. I want to thank you again for the commendation letter you presented to the chief. He let me read it. You were very generous in your comments," "I meant them and you deserved them," Jason said. "Your investigation was exemplary and now Mr. Kramer is behind bars." "Have you heard the latest news regarding the Brady case?" O'Reilly asked. "No I haven't. What is it?" "In the civil court the restitution judgment for Mr. Brady has been set at $2.2 million dollars! Mr. Kramer is having trouble raising the money. It seems that some of the criminals he defended are not paying their bills now that he's also in the penitentiary."

One of them not paying his bill was Marvin the "Mole," the criminal Kramer had unsuccessfully defended in LA. Unfortunately for Mr. Kramer they were both assigned to the same prison. The "Mole" represented a constant threat to Kramer and he was terrified.

"He may even have to sell his Beverly Hills estate to pay his bills," O'Reilly said. Jason was elated. "I hope that happens. Money will never be enough to repay Mr. Brady for the loss of his wife and son." They chatted for a few more minutes and then hung up. Jason told Stephanie about the restitution settlement. "I hope Mr. Kramer's career is over and he becomes destitute," she said. "He's one of the most despicable men I have ever encountered." In so many ways so am I Jason thought. You just don't realize it.

# Chapter 41

THEY ARRIVED IN San Diego's Lindbergh field later that night and drove straight to Jason's home. He took her down to his spectacular wine cellar. There he selected a Vintage 1992 Peter Michael Winery "Les Pavots" Red Table wine to enjoy with Stephanie. "Before I die I want to drink up my best vintages with your help." he said. "We need to share some of them with friends Jason," she said. She hoped that the Goldins would join them for dinner in La Jolla before Jason died. She mentioned it as a possibility to Jason. "I know you would like that to happen, but Valerie would be torn. I don't think she would come," he said. "Why have I created so much anguish in her life? She is such an honorable and ethical person. When I am gone please tell her how much I secretly admired her. It's a shame I haven't come out and told her that. Now I am afraid it's too late," he remarked. "It's never too late," Stephanie replied. "Creating and main-taining friendships mean more to me than just making money. It's possible to have both. You can still try to have both," she said. "Valerie has both and so do I. My highest priority now is to make you happy. You will be happier and you will relieve yourself of a great deal of guilt if you would only apologize to Valerie. But it has to be sincere." That was the hard part, he thought. After all these years of perpetuating lies and deceptions, could he change and be sincere? The best he could manage to say was. "I can try Stephanie. I can try."

It didn't matter now that Jason's option strategies were working. He was going to die. He decided to repent and give current and timely option seminars three times a week in the Kaplan office. Now they were well attended by the investment advisors including Valerie. They appreciated his candid comments and advice. Those following his up to date option trades were making money. Barry Greenberg was also attending some of Jason's classes. He was intrigued by the many mathematical nuances involved in option strategies. Despite Valerie's fears, he had not turned over any of his account to Jason even before Jason's cancer was discovered. He had remained loyal to Valerie and she appreciated his loyalty. "Valerie the leverage advantages of option trades are incredible, but you have to get them right or you can lose money on a regular basis," Barry remarked. "I'm learning a great deal from Jason Gianelli. He's a very savvy option trader." Valerie mused. He would not be an option trader much longer. He was obviously declining rapidly. Yet he continued the option training sessions for two more months. He wasn't out to steal clients anymore. In fact he showed a sincere desire to help his colleagues. It was a refreshing change brought on by metastatic cancer. Most co-workers felt he was trying to assuage his guilt. In truth that's exactly what he was doing. He couldn't make up for all of his unethical actions. They were spread out over too many years. At least he could try to make a difference in their lives before he died.

He sent out letters to his clients stating he would no longer be available to manage their accounts after the first of April 2011. He offered to refer them to his co-workers and asked them to make appointments with him for his recommendations. He had interviewed all the other 15 investment advisors in the firm. In analyzing their investment strategies he had focused on their last five years of returns That time span included the bear market that started in 2007 and lasted until late February 2009. Valerie clearly held the best annualized return and he planned on referring most of his clients to her. Unfortunately he could not refer any of them to John Davenport. He was dead. Jason knew he had caused his suicide. He would try to make amends for that in other ways.

He made an appointment to see Valerie in her office. After exchanging polite greetings, Valerie gave Jason a wary look. "Why did you want to see me Jason?" she inquired. "Valerie I want to refer some of my best clients to you. If they agree, will you accept them?" he asked. "Jason I appreciate your offer. I will be happy to manage their accounts if they're willing to accept my investment style. They will be disappointed in my results though. You have to warn them that I'm no Jason Gianelli, the man with the golden option strategies and shorting techniques," she said. Jason was flattered and thanked Valerie for her kind comments.

"Valerie I know I've been a terrible rival. I hope your added commissions from my referred clients will help counteract some of your bad feelings toward me," he said. "I'm still struggling over our intense rivalry Jason. It's been emotionally crippling for me at times. You've seemed to take it in stride, but I've suffered." He would never quite grasp the intensity of her suffering. His only major setback had been the loss of the Friedman account and it was an account he never deserved. "Well please do your best for my former clients," he said. "I wish you success in managing their accounts." With that he stood up and abruptly left her office.

Was this finally the turning point in their relationship Valerie wondered? Perhaps it was but not completely. He still hadn't apologized for all the anguish he had generated in her life. And, she thought, he probably never would.

# Chapter 42

ROBERT KAPLAN CALLED a general meeting for his entire staff to discuss Jason's status. "By now you are all aware that Jason Gianelli is dying," he said. "I know many of you harbor a grudge against Jason. I want to open this meeting up to a discussion as to how we should deal with Jason's situation. As you know, despite the pain his cancer is causing him, he's been holding three option training sessions a week in this office for the past two months. Most of you have been attending them. He's been sharing his best current option strategies with you and some of you have been making money following his recommendations. Today I received a call from him. He told me that he will no longer be able to return to the office. His condition has deteriorated to the point that he is no longer able to participate in further training sessions. He has been hospitalized today. I don't think he has much time left before he dies. I want to open up this meeting for a discussion as to how we should deal with Jason's pre-terminal condition. Are there any comments or ideas?" he asked.

A chorus of unfavorable comments gushed out from the audience. He heard comments such as. "I don't want to do anything for him. He has always thought he was better than me." Someone else said. "I agree. He never offered to help me until these last two months. When I had attended his older option seminars, he would often belittle me in front of clients." Another employee said. "He was always touting his superior investment returns. He tried to steal my clients. I never trusted him." "Yes, his option seminars were designed to steal clients. I have never trusted him either," chimed in another person in the audience.

After an additional litany of accusations filled the room, Valerie finally spoke up. "All of us have had our reasons to dislike and distrust Jason. He is now dying and will no longer be coming to the office. Why don't we give him a chance to apologize to us before he dies?" she asked. Someone in the audience said. "What makes you think he will apologize, Valerie?" "Maybe he won't apologize," she responded. "But by not giving him that opportunity reflects poorly on each of us. I think we need to rise above Jason's shortcomings and our resentments. At least we can feel good about ourselves if we do that," she added. There was silence in the room. Her statements had caused people to reflect and measure their feelings. Valerie broke the silence by saying. "Please join me in paying him a visit. We can go together or separately." There was absolute silence. Not a single person volunteered to go.

Robert Kaplan was surprised by the intensity of the indictments against Jason. "I want to remind you that Jason will leave a legacy of being the best investment advisor this firm has ever produced," he commented. Someone in the audience responded saying. "He will also leave a legacy of being the most reprehensible advisor in this firm." There was an atmosphere of bitterness that pervaded the room. "We can't send him a get well card," someone commented. "I vote for sending him a die well card signed by all of us," someone else in the audience said.

Valerie was shocked but also validated. There were people in the audience who seemed to hate Jason as much as she did. "Some of you have met my client Stephanie Shea," Valerie said. "She is also my best friend. She is a wonderful, kind and generous person and is also in love with Jason. She married Jason in a private wedding ceremony over one month ago." Looks of disbelief filled the room. Valerie continued. "Her first husband died of metastatic colon cancer. She will shortly lose Jason to cancer too. She is not aware of the virulent feelings so many of you have toward Jason. I don't want her to know. There is little hope for a pleasant ending to Jason's life. In his adverse dealings with us, he has in effect denied himself our blessings," she concluded.

Robert Kaplan was about to end the meeting when Valerie interjected. "I have something else to tell you. This was passed on to me in confidence from Stephanie. Please don't let it slip out if you visit Jason. A $100,000 anonymous check has been deposited into the bank account of Mrs. Laura Davenport, John Davenport's wife. It came from Jason. He has also set up two college fund accounts for Tommy and Marsha, her two children. He deposited $20,000 into each account. Jason asked Stephanie to deliver two adorable Cocker Spaniel puppies to Tommy and Marsha over the weekend. Stephanie described how thrilled they were with their squealing little pups and how they blurted out their thanks. She watched them cuddle and hug the squirming little puppies as joy sparkled in their eyes. Stephanie also said Laura's face just beamed and her smile was radiant She was was so grateful and glad to see her children happy.

"We can choose to be cynical and think Laura and her children deserve the money and attention. Many of us feel that Jason was responsible for John's eventual suicide. Or we can at least modify our thinking toward the concept that Jason's gifts are magnanimous. I personally think he did these things because he was feeling guilty. But he didn't have to do any of them and they will certainly help Laura, Tommy and Marsha. Perhaps Jason does have a heart after all. It just won't be beating much longer," she said.

At the close of Valerie's comments Robert Kaplan ended the meeting. People milled around the office discussing their reactions to Valerie's remarks. Some reluctantly said they might visit Jason. Others were adamant and said they would never pay him a visit. Valerie no longer cared. She had expressed her personal feelings and her position on the matter. She wanted to comfort Stephanie and give Jason a chance to apologize for all the grief he had caused everyone in the office over the years. She was still struggling over her willingness to forgive him.

# Chapter 43

THE FOLLOWING DAY Valerie paid Jason a hospital visit. She was disappointed to learn that so far no one from the office outside of Robert Kaplan had visited Jason. Stephanie quickly rose from Jason's bedside chair and opened her arms to give Valerie a warm hug. "Thanks for coming, Valerie," she said.

Jason looked gaunt and despondent. He looked up at Valerie, "Yes, thanks for coming," he said. He was grateful for her visit. Those prophetic words of a co-worker during Judy Gianelli's rant were haunting him. He vividly recalled the statement. I hope when you die you will be alone and miserable. It was agonizing to die without friends. He reached down to pet a whimpering Brady who looked so sad as he looked longingly into Jason's sunken eyes wondering what was happening to him. Brady cared, but his former clients seemingly didn't. Not a single one had visited him. How could they be so unfeeling. He had made them so much money.

"Have you seen any of the clients I referred to you," he asked. "Yes, quite a few," Valerie said. Jason's face twisted in anguish. A momentary flicker of rage surged from his eyes. He asked himself. Why weren't they visiting him? He wasn't dead yet. "They express their regret in losing you, Jason. They realize I won't be able to match your returns."

Jason likened his former clients to rats scurrying around the deck of a sinking ship looking for ways to escape. Couldn't they face the reality of his death? He had been so full of life and enthusiasm. Were they afraid of their own mortality and vulnerability?

With tears in his eyes he gazed up into Valerie's face and said. "Valerie I know I've caused you a great deal of pain over the last two decades. I admit some of it was intentional. I'm deeply ashamed of myself. I'm so sorry Valerie. I apologize for all the stress I've caused in your life. Please accept my apology. Will you do that for me?" His voice was weak and he looked so pitiful. This was no longer the dynamic and powerful option king who tried to dominate her over the years. No, he was a dying and decaying man pleading for forgiveness. Cancer had humbled him. His days of glory and preeminence were behind him. Valerie paused before responding. He had to be dying before he could offer her an apology she thought. He wouldn't have done it otherwise.

She pictured herself standing in the center of the labyrinth and looking out toward the vast Pacific Ocean. There she had experienced a deep reverence for life and realized her relative insignificance in the world. She had adamantly rejected Dr. Chang's proposal to consider walking with Jason through the labyrinth. That opportunity to seek harmony with him was lost. Now he was reaching out to her and she could no longer reject him. She had to make a decision and a choice. She turned to him and said quietly. "Thank you, Jason. I accept your apology." She gently touched his shoulder. But she was still flawed. She was unable to say I forgive you. With that thought lingering in her mind she excused herself and left the hospital.

Stephanie gave Jason a hug and a gentle kiss. "Thank you for apologizing to Valerie. She needed to hear that from you," she said. He nodded a yes and said. "But she hasn't forgiven me Stephanie. Did you notice that?" he asked. "Yes I did. She's so conflicted. I think she left in order to contemplate your apology. She will probably meditate and pray over it. The La Jolla Center for Integrative Medicine has provided her with ways to deal with stress and confusion. She's struggling with her emotions in the same way you're struggling with yours." She bent down and giving him a kiss said. "I love you Jason." He looked up with gratitude. She was the only person left in his life who truly cared about him. "I love you too Stephanie." His eyes glazed over in pain. He called the nurse for more pain medication. After it took effect, he said. "I'm so tired. I think I'll try to get some sleep." His confession to Valerie and the debilitating effects of metastatic cancer had left him exhausted. But Valerie's acceptance of his apology also gave him some relief. He soon fell into a deep sleep.

When Jason woke up Stephanie gave him a gentle hug and looked into his eyes. "You had a long sleep. Do you feel better?" she asked. "Yes, but I am so tormented by all the grief I've caused Valerie and my office co-workers over the years. Valerie is so honest and forthright. I haven't treated her fairly," he said. "But you told me you were in competition with her for clients and for better investment returns. Isn't that what was driving you to be the best in the firm?" she asked. "Yes, but I was also unethical in so many ways. I did try to steal her clients and the clients of others in the office," he said. "I was driven to succeed without regard for the feelings of my co-workers. I wanted to be the vice president of the firm by proving to everyone that I was clearly the most outstanding investment advisor." "But you are the best," she replied. "No, I was the best. Now I'm nothing. I'm despised by everyone in the firm. Robert Kaplan hates my ethics. He knew I was dishonest and devious regarding the Friedmans' account. He never would have granted me the vice presidency. In truth I didn't deserve it but Valerie does. Then there's the issue of John Davenport's suicide, a suicide I caused. When I took away his clients he hung himself. I didn't even go his funeral. I was the only one from the office absent."

Stephanie was deeply troubled by his confession. He was revealing malevolent aspects of his character that he had hidden from her. She was greatly distressed but her overriding love for him remained intact. Except for her he would die alone and miserable. He had been so generous and loving to her, and yet apparently so devious and spiteful to Valerie and others. Her emotions were twisted. Valerie and Jason were the two most important people in her life and one of them, her husband, would shortly die. She would again be a widow and it would devastate her.

His condition worsened the following day. Stephanie was alarmed and called Father Flanagan asking him to pay Jason a visit. Jason was now on a continuous intravenous morphine drip to control his pain. He was still conscious and was talking with Stephanie when Father Flanagan entered the room. The priest proceeded to talk and then pray quietly with Jason. He asked Jason to confess his sins. There was a look of dismay and concern on Jason's face. He knew how egregious and plentiful his sins had been over the years. He questioned in his own mind if even a generous, loving God could forgive him of all his sins. He finally relented and confessed. The priest laid his hands on Jason's forehead and said. "Through this holy anointing may the Lord in his love and mercy help you with the grace of the Holy Spirit." Next taking Jason's hands he said. "May the Lord who freed you from sin save you and raise you up." With that Jason said "amen" and looked relieved. Soon the priest left the room.

Just then Valerie walked into his room. Jason briefly smiled. "Thank you for coming to see me again Valerie," he said. He meant it. He no longer viewed her as a rival. "Jason I want you to know how much your apology meant to me. I have had so much resentment toward you over the years. Your apology has helped to erase some of it," she said. "I wish I could erase all of it Valerie but I know that's too much to expect. I just want you to hear this again. I sincerely apologize for all the distress I've caused you. You have every right to be angry with me. After I am dead, I hope you will let your anger fade and eventually disappear." He began to cry. Valerie reached down and took both of his hands into hers. "Jason I want to thank you again for your apology. After leaving you yesterday, I meditated and prayed. I feel much better now." She looked into his eyes and said. "I forgive you Jason. Do you hear me? I forgive you." A look of relief crossed Jason's face. Gazing up into her eyes he said. "Thank you Valerie. I've needed your forgiveness. It will help me have a more peaceful death."

Stephanie was so grateful for Valerie's statement of forgiveness. She gave Valerie a hug and whispered thank you into her ear. Valerie was satisfied. She walked slowly toward the door and then turned around to say, "Good bye Jason." Valerie waited in the hospital hallway outside of Jason's room. Inside his room Stephanie was softly crying as she cradled Jason's head. It wasn't long before a nurse scurried past Valerie and entered his room. Then she heard Stephanie sobbing and she knew Jason had died. As she looked into the room confirming Jason's death, she whispered to herself. "Yes Jason I forgive you, but I will never forget you."

Please visit the author's online sites:

www.walterjensenmd.com

www.facebook.com/walterjensenmd

www.twitter.com/@walterjensenmd

or email him at:

wjtennis@cox.net

CPSIA information can be obtained at www.ICGtesting.com
Printed in the USA
BVOW01s1957030614

355278BV00001B/168/P

9 781940 745220